Praise

for THE SHELLY GALE SERIES

*"Lizzy is an excellent writer! Her books are easy to read, but **the mysteries are written so well that the reader is left guessing throughout the story until the reveal at the very end.**"*

—Becky Bowers

*"I love reading the Shelly Gale series. I've been waiting for this book to develop! **This Christian series is well-written and will keep you on the edge of your seat.** Trust me, you won't want to put the book down."*

—Cheryl Isom

*"I love reading Lizzy Armentrout's Shelly Gale mysteries because she does a great job of making me feel like I'm really there on her adventures. You can clearly picture every detail of the stories. She also does **a great job of keeping me guessing who's done it until the very end of the book. I highly recommend everyone read these books.**"*

—Mary Tackett

*"**The perfect balance between all things Christian and Murder Mystery...**"*

—Christian Murder Mystery

*"**The action was fast-paced and there were enough twists and turns to keep me guessing...**"*

—Christian Mystery

LIZZY ARMENTROUT

A DECEPTIVE SPIRIT

A Deceptive Spirit, *A Shelly Gale Mystery, Book 3*
by Lizzy Armentrout

Published by

FSP
FIRST STEPS
PUBLISHING

First Steps Publishing
PO Box 571
Gleneden Beach, OR 97388
publish@firststepspublishing.com

Book design copyright ©2025 by First Steps Publishing. All rights reserved.
Cover and Interior design and layout by Suzanne Fyhrie Parrott
Images: *Tobacco Barn*; ©Suzanne Parrott; Midjourney.com

ISBN-13:   978-1-945146-62-6 (hb)
            978-1-945146-61-9 (pb)
            978-1-945146-63-3 (epub)

1. Fiction / Christian / Suspense; 2. Fiction / Crime; 3. Fiction / Mystery & Detective / Cozy / General; 4. Fiction / Family Life / General; 5. Social Science / Human Trafficking

Mystery suspense / small town / human trafficking / crime drama / family life / North Carolina / cozy

10 9 8 7 6 5 4 3 2 1

Printed in the
United States of America

LIZZY ARMENTROUT

A DECEPTIVE SPIRIT

FSP

FIRST STEPS PUBLISHING

For the Author Seeking a Solid Foundation

SHELLY GALE MYSTERY SERIES

A Vengeful Spirit
A Covetous Spirit
A Deceptive Spirit

Author, Lizzy Armentrout

This third book is dedicated to the two people who have given of their time and energy to help me make this the best possible version of this story.

First, I dedicate it to David Wisniewski, my brother from another mother. He gave me so many insights and was a huge sounding board for me as I brainstormed different scenes in this story. Not only has he helped me with all three books, but he's also helped me and my family in so many ways throughout the years. Love you, Dave!

Secondly, this book is dedicated to Angelia Cook who was my biggest encourager. When I was injured and unable to write, she was the one who kept the storyline alive and would ask me about the characters. She herself has many things on her plate, but she took the time to be a reader as I wrote and would give me insights on what parts of the story made sense or didn't. She is one of my best friends, and I appreciate her being a part of my life and this book. This book would not be here without her help. Love you, Cook!

In Gratitude

First, I must thank my husband for prodding me to keep going even when I really just wanted to quit writing. He just wouldn't let me stop!

Secondly, thank you to all my readers. You will never know how much it boosts me when you tell me what your favorite character is or what your favorite scene is. I hope you enjoy this book as much as the first two.

And lastly, but most importantly, thank you to my Lord and Savior for changing my life and giving me so many blessings.

Chapter One

August 20th, 3:30 pm

It had been a frantic day getting her fourteen-year-old adopted son, Tucker, out the door to his freshman football practice, taking the dog to the vet for his annual check-up, and going by the Social Security Administration to change her name to her married name. That stop, even though frustrating due to the usual bureaucracy, put a huge smile on her face when she held her new card and saw, "Shelly Gale Rogers."

She had just finished the best chocolate and peanut butter milkshake on the planet from Dogs-n-Taters as she turned into the Pilotview Mall and looked for a parking space in the crowded lot. *Great! It looks like everyone else waited until the last minute to do their back-to-school shopping like me. Oh! There's a spot over there!* Seeing a spot right next to the sidewalk, Shelly thanked the Lord for opening one up for her but then yelped when a rusty, white van blew its horn at her as it pulled in.

The nerve of some people! Oh well! Not worth fighting over. Good thing Curly's not here; he'd have a thing to say over that broken taillight! She finally found her parking spot in the back under a tree and quickly started working on her shopping list.

In a couple of hours, Shelly had found several good sales and was almost done with Tucker's school shopping. She groaned as she entered the slow-moving, long line to check out at Belk's department store. It barely moved several inches and then came to a complete stop. Shifting her merchandise from her right to her left arm, she smiled at the baby in front of her to keep from screaming in frustration at the line. His bright blue eyes and red hair brought back memories of Tucker.

Tucker had really grown over the summer, transitioning from a goofy middle schooler to a gangly teen. She remembered that fateful night when her young student became an orphan. A year later, she and her husband, Curly, who had now been promoted to lieutenant in the Pilotview Police Department, had adopted their wonderful son.

As she smiled and waved at the baby, she overheard a security guard's walkie-talkie squealing as he rushed by. Right when he reached the doors, a series of beeps came over the intercom followed by an announcement, "We are initiating a Code Orange. We need all customers and employees to evacuate the mall immediately."

Oh, this can't be good. Lord, I have no idea what a Code Orange is, but I've seen that same look on Curly's face many times when things are really, really bad. Please help us!

She threw her selections onto the ground and started making her way to the same exit where the security guard was holding the door to help people exit. As she tried to make her way through the river of people that was becoming bottlenecked at the doors, she saw an elderly lady struggling to maneuver her walker through the anxious mob. "Let me help you, Ma'am," she offered as she started leading the lady.

"Aren't you just the sweetest thing! I've never heard tell of a Code Orange before. Do you know what that might be?" the lady nervously said while pulling on her string of pearls as Shelly continued to gently prod her toward the door.

"No, Ma'am, I don't, but it must be something serious for them to evacuate the entire mall, so we best be trying to get out of here as quickly as we can." People bumped and jostled them from all sides. It was all she could do to protect the older woman while maintaining their movement toward the security guard. Suddenly, a huge, muscular man stopped, smiled, and just picked up the lady and her walker and carried her through the confusion and out the doors.

Whew! Who was that man? An angel? Thank you, Lord, for sending help for her! Now, to get myself out of here. Trying not to fall in the middle of all the pushing and shoving, she worked her way to the door. What had been a calm, peaceful place just a few minutes earlier was now complete pandemonium. Not only were people screaming and crying, but the intercom kept repeating the same warning along with sirens and alarms squawking. Then, a horrific explosion erupted, shaking the floor and causing several racks to topple around her.

She had just made it through the door when an elbow to the ribs knocked her down. The last things she remembered were the sensation of falling, along with hearing explosions and screaming!

Chapter Two

Earlier that day

The station bustled with all sorts of activity as Lieutenant Greg Rogers, Curly to his family and friends, waded through the mountain of reports and paperwork that had piled up while he was in the Caribbean helping keep Tim and Nicole out of jail while on their honeymoon. Stopping to stretch, he rubbed his neck and couldn't help but smile while thinking of Shelly and how beautiful she looked this morning as she slept while he quietly left for his shift. *This marriage thing is way better than I had ever thought it could be. I know one thing—we're gonna have to start looking for a bigger place. With her taking the year off school, we can't stay in the church apartment, and my place sure isn't big enough for three people and a dog. Guess we'll talk about it tonight.*

Returning his attention to the reports, the intercom went off. "Lieutenant, your brother is on line one for ya. Do ya want to take it, or should I take a message?" Sheila asked as he heard the annoying pop of chewing gum.

"I'll go ahead and take it. Thanks, Sheila." He punched the button for line one and spent several minutes catching up with his younger brother, Chad. Listening to him excitedly talking about his upcoming graduation made Curly grin with pride. "Sure wish

Dad was able to be here to see this. Can't tell ya how proud I am of you."

"Me too, Curly."

"Be sure to text me all the details for the graduation so I can get it on my calendar. I want to make sure we are all there to cheer you on. By the way, it's perfect timing for you to graduate. Officer Joyello just took a job down at the Outer Banks. So, we'll have an entry-level position opening in just a few weeks. Be sure to go onto our website and put your app in."

"I'll do that now, Curly, thanks!"

After catching up on the upcoming football season and their favorite team, the Panthers, he finally ended the call and dug back into the ever-waiting paperwork.

As Curly read the police blotter for the town's weekly staff meeting, he groaned as the unmistakable gravelly voice of Jed McManus drifted down the hallway. *Great! Just what I don't need! An hour spent chasing down some imaginary crime that Jed has cooked up just to get some attention! Lord, give me patience, please!*

Curly sighed as he stood. *Best to get this over with.* Leaving his pile of work behind, he strode out to meet Jed. Turning the corner to the front lobby, he overheard Sheila teasing him, "Now, Jed. Ya know I think yer chicken stew is mighty fine. But it can't shake a stick at Miz Opal's. There's jest no denyin' that hers is the best in the county, maybe even the state!"

"Humph! Miz Opal don't know nuthin' bout makin' chicken stew. She don't even use no Texas Pete. Land's sakes! How in tarnation can ya call it chicken stew without Texas Pete in it, girl?'"

Jed argued, as he hitched his pants up even higher on his pot belly. "Now ya listen to me, girl, the best way to make chicken stew…" Seeing the lieutenant had entered the lobby area, Jed raised his hand and waved off the argument with, "Oh, ya jest ne'er mind. Jest sees ya'll come on out to my chicken stew in jest a couple a months on the first Saturday in October. Now, I has some important bizness for Curly, scuse me, Lieutenant Rogers."

"Hello, Jed, what can I do for you on this fine day?" Curly asked, as he leaned against the front counter and gave Sheila a playful wink.

Jed turned to Curly and continued, "Well, I hear tell congratulations are in order. First, for getting a promotion when you solved that boy of yers mama's murder but then fer goin' and gettin' married. Boy! What's wrong with ya? There went all yer freedom AND yer money!"

Sheila popped a bubble, then laughed as Jed continued, "I didn't come all the ways over here jest ta trade recipes with this here girl. I have a matter that calls fer some detectin' and I figured ya were my best shot since ya were a detective jest a few weeks back."

Chuckling, Curly motioned for Jed to proceed him down the hallway to his office, "Go on in and sit a spell, Jed, and tell me what's been going on at your place." He led him into his tiny office and got him seated. "Want some coffee?"

Looking around at the office that only had room for a desk and two chairs, Jed asked, "I thought ya got yerself a promotion? Don't that come with a bigger office? This is so tiny a person can hardly breathe in here." Before Curly could answer, he continued, "Never mind 'bout that. I got me a serious situation goin' on at my place, son. I need for you ta find out who's stealing all my food!" Jed hollered as he thumped his fist on the edge of Curly's desk.

"Why would someone steal your food, Jed?" Curly leaned back and tried to stretch his legs out to get comfortable since he knew Jed was notorious for making up all kinds of attention-grabbing, non-existent crimes.

"I don't KNOW why! That's what we pay taxes fer! Fer ya'll to do some detectin'! I swarmy! Barney Fife could do a better job than this here police department!" Jed thundered in his gravelly smoker's voice as he went into a coughing fit.

Curly sat up and cleared his throat. "Mr. McManus, why don't you start from the beginning and catch me up?"

As he listened to Jed's story, he realized that he might actually have a legitimate crime this time. "Slow down a minute. Let me get all this down in my notes. You say you went grocery shopping last Friday and filled your freezer chest full of all kinds of meat. Correct?" At Jed's nod he asked, "Was the freezer locked?"

"Locked? What on earth fer, boy? I ain't never had ta lock a thing in all my days a livin' here. I just want my meat back! Some fool kids probably did it ta pull a prank or somethin'. They're all always gettin' inta trouble. If ya ask me, parents today…"

Curly hastened to interrupt before he started into his favorite topic of how awful today's parents are, "Tell ya what, Jed. I'm gonna ride on out to your place and take a look at what's going on. I'm truly baffled that someone would steal your food."

"Bout time ya did somethin' round here 'cept go on cruises!" Jed grumbled as he followed Curly out to the front lobby.

"Jed, go ahead on home. I'm going to check in with Sheila so I should be about five minutes behind you." Curly watched the older man exit the building, walk over to his faded, rusty, red 2000 Ford Ranger truck and back out. After seeing that he had exited the parking lot without difficulty, Curly turned to get his things.

Stealing a freezer full of food. Usually, he complains of trespassers or kids making loud noises. Surely this isn't anything serious.

Chapter Three

The ride to Jed's place was so quick that Curly didn't even have time to hear the latest sports update. Jed and his wife lived in the same brick rancher that Jed's dad had built after he had retired from tobacco farming. He couldn't help but admire the long, windy, paved drive lined with red crepe myrtle trees.

As he reached out to knock on the door, Jed yanked it open and barked out, "Took ya long enough. What'd ya do? Go to Winston first? Well, yer here now. Come on out back of the garage. That's where I've had this here chest freezer for the last ten years. I ain't never had no trouble a'tall with anyone ever stealing anything from it before!"

Standing inside the garage, Jed threw out his arm and pointed at a rusty Whirlpool chest freezer with an open lid.

Pulling on his latex gloves, Curly carefully investigated the open and quite empty freezer. He then opened his bag and took out his fingerprint kit. "I doubt I'll find any prints other than yours, Jed, but it's best to be sure." Curly dusted all the places he thought a thief might have touched but only found one print, and it was on the handle. "I'm pretty sure this is your print, Jed. To be sure, I'll need to get your prints for comparison. Next time you are in town, stop in and tell Sheila I said you needed to get printed, and she'll take care of it for you." He then walked around the property, looking for anything out of the ordinary.

"I'm sorry, Jed, but I just don't see any evidence here at all that I can use to track your meat down." At the expected harrumph, he went on, "However, this a priority, and I will get my brother, Chad, out here to go door to door. Hopefully someone saw something that will give us a lead. In the meantime, you need to refill your freezer and install a hidden camera for us to catch the thief in action," he encouraged as he packed his things and walked to the car.

Hiking up his pants while spitting on the ground, Jed complained, "It jest figures that ya'll wouldn't be no help a'tall." He threw up his hand and slammed the door as he went back into the house.

Well then! With Jed, you just never have to wonder how he feels about anything! Curly called into the station and updated Sheila on his status and told her to call Chad and get him started on the door-to-door. Deciding it was time to grab a bite to eat, he drove over to the local hot dog stand, Dogs-n-Taters, since Shelly was at the mall finishing up last-minute school shopping, and Tucker was at football practice. As usual, Dogs-n-Taters didn't have any open seats, so he leaned against the wall with all the others who were waiting and got caught up on all the local gossip he missed while he and Shelly had been on the cruise. Finally, a seat became available at the counter next to his pastor, so he quickly grabbed it.

"Well, hey there, Curly! How's it feel to be a married man?" Pastor Thomas asked before taking the next bite of his chili dog.

Curly smiled at the question he had already answered ten times that morning and replied, "Better than I had ever imagined or dared to dream. We just wish you had been there to perform the ceremony. I'm glad I caught up with you. We want to have a ceremony here at home in our church in front of our friends and family. Would you be willing to officiate?" They discussed the logistics of the ceremony and dates as Curly ordered, and the pastor finished his lunch. "Before you go, Pastor, I've got a strange case that happened just this morning. I was wondering if you knew of any new folk who might've moved into town?"

The pastor took a sip of his sweet tea and thought a moment. Shaking his head he answered, "No, I don't think so. Oh! Wait! It's not what you're probably looking for, but while ya'll were gone, we had an older fella move into town from out in Texas to be closer to his daughter and grandkids. His name is Alan, and I'm sure ya'll will become fast friends because he's a retired state trooper. He moved into the Watt's old place out on Coon Hollow Road. You should stop by and introduce yourself."

"A retired state trooper, huh? I just might do that." When the waitress laid the pastor's check down, Curly quickly reached over and picked it up. "Let me get this. You do so much for us that it's the least I can do."

Clapping Curly on the back, the pastor told him he would be praying for him and made his farewell. Curly decided that since he didn't have anything except more paperwork waiting on him that after he finished his ice cream sundae, he would just head on over to Coon Hollow Road and meet Pilotview's newest resident. *Maybe he'll have some ideas on this stolen freezer food!*

Chapter Four

Breathe. Just breathe. You can make it. Just hold on a little longer. You're almost there. Tucker strained as he ran the last lap for football practice. In the ninety-five-degree heat that had ninety percent humidity, practice had been miserable. Still, he was so excited at not only making the team but being a starter that he couldn't even complain about the heat. Seeing his buddy, Marc Taylor, crossing the line to finish motivated him to bear down and put on a final boost to catch up. A few seconds later, he finished right behind Marc and ran to the water cooler to get some much-needed water.

"Hey, Marc! You and Dave wanna come over for some head-to-head Assassin's Creed? Mama Shelly already said it'd be okay 'cuz she'll be there."

"Sure! Let me give my mom a call." After Marc quickly called and got permission, they both turned to see if Dave would join them.

"I just texted and asked. Mom said it's okay, but she can't give me a ride over there and get back to her office in time. Ya think yer mom could give me a ride, Tuck?"

"I'm sure it'll be okay. Let me text and double-check though. Why don't I see if both of ya'll can just ride home with me?" He quickly shot off a message while continuing, "She's school shopping, so it might be a bit 'fore I hear from her. Thank goodness she didn't make me go with her! I hate shopping, especially school shopping!"

Coach Waddell lumbered over to lightly punch all three boys on their arms. "Hey, Tuck! I liked those moves out there today! Keep working, and you'll be the fastest running back in our region!" The coach was an imposing six-foot-three-inch man who had to weigh over three hundred pounds, but the kids quickly figured out that while he looked intimidating, he was really cool to hang out with. "I found out last night that all ya'll are in my Social Studies class this year."

Chuckling at their cheers and high-fives, he continued, "That means I'll have my eye on ya. Since you're eighth graders, I expect all ya'll to be leaders and set a good example for the rest of the team and the school. "

Tucker punched the coach on the arm and joked, "What? We can't go partyin'? Man! You ruin everything!"

"Ha! Ha! Like I'm worried about that with the parents you have. Between having a police officer for a dad and a teacher for a mom, you're the last one I'll be worrying about because they would kill ya before I could even think about kicking your tail for doing anything stupid. Hey, I don't see your rides yet, so why don't all ya'll help me and Coach Aram put up the equipment?"

When Tucker saw his mom hadn't replied to his text, he shrugged and agreed to help his favorite coach. He had to laugh watching him and the assistant coach, Aram Nassad, walking next to each other. Aram only came up to the Coach's shoulder and was so thin that they always teased him that a strong wind would blow him away. Despite being so thin, all the guys had noticed that he was strong, and it looked like he spent hours working out in the gym.

It seemed like everything had changed in his life since that day he found his mom murdered on the kitchen floor. Now he had Shelly for a mom and Curly for a dad. He had expected that he would still be at Lighthouse Christian School, but after praying about it, his new parents decided Shelly would take a year off from teaching so she could focus on being a wife and mother since it had all happened so quickly. Since Shelly wasn't teaching at the Christian school any longer, they could not afford to send him. This meant that he was now enrolled at Walnut Park Middle School, known as the Park to the locals.

Having grown up in a Christian school, Tucker wasn't sure what to expect. He had only been to practices, but so far, it wasn't as bad as he had expected. Several of the guys were in his youth group at church, and they had invited him to join the Christian club at school. He had also been asked to do things he knew were wrong. That had also happened at the Christian school. Yet, he was pleasantly surprised when he got his schedule and saw that he had two teachers who were faithful church members.

"Well, guys, that's all of it. Thanks for all your help." Looking around the parking lot, the coach asked, "Who is your ride? Have to say I'm a bit surprised, Tuck, 'cause your mom is usually here to watch at least a part of practice."

Tucker nodded in agreement, rechecked his phone, and still didn't see a text. He sent her another one and then called his new dad. "Hey, Cur…ugh, I mean, Dad. Sheesh! I'm sorry. I don't think I'm ever gonna get used to all these new names!"

Curly wiped the chocolate syrup off his chin and chuckled,

"No problem, son, it's all good. Have to say this is a nice surprise. What's up? You usually just text me."

Tucker quickly explained that he didn't have a ride home and hadn't been able to contact Shelly. He then asked if his buddies could come home with him.

"You know I have no problem with Dave and Marc hanging out at our house, but let me see what's going on with your mom first. Now that you bring it up, I just realized I haven't heard from her all day, and I usually get at least one text from her. I'm sure it's nothing. Probably just in a dead spot at the mall. I tell you what. I'll come get ya'll. I'll be there in fifteen minutes, and by then, I should have an answer for you." After ending the call, he threw enough money down on the counter to cover his bill and hustled out to his black Ford Explorer that he had been given when he got the promotion to lieutenant. As he headed over to the Park, he repeatedly kept calling Shelly.

Lord, this is very unusual. She would never be out of touch with Tucker. Maybe she just forgot to charge her phone last night. Please let that be all it is.

Chapter Five

If only Shelly had known that morning that her day would go off the rails, she would have hugged Tucker and Curly even tighter and not let them go. She loved being both a wife and a mother and enjoyed making breakfast, seeing Curly off to work, and taking Tucker to the school for football practice. Continuing her morning routine, Shelly returned to the apartment, started a load of wash, and took Max for a much-needed walk before taking him to the vet for his check-up. Since she returned, he'd been extremely clingy, so she was trying to give him special love and attention.

Earlier, the radio ran several advertisements announcing that numerous stores at the mall had huge markdowns for back-to-school, so she figured she would get the rest of Tucker's things while he was at practice for the day. After getting Max some water, she texted her friend Nicole and invited her to join her for a girl's day of shopping.

"Girl, I would love to, but some of us must work! Enjoy shopping while I am sitting in training meetings all day! I AM JEALOUS!" Laughing at her reply, Shelly loaded Max in the car for his vet appointment, got her things together, and proceeded to the vet. Since she was starting so early, she hoped to finish everything in time to watch Tucker's afternoon practice.

Having hit all of Tucker's favorite stores, she only had a few things left on her list. She headed into Belk and was thrilled to find they had marked their junior boys' clothing down thirty percent. With her arms full, she realized she needed to hurry to make it to the Park in time to catch practice. She couldn't help but grin at how excited he had been at being named a starter for the team. Having played in the town's youth football leagues his whole life, he had a huge advantage. As she walked toward the checkout, she couldn't resist adding a few additional items for Curly. *These prices are awesome. I'll have to come back this evening with Nicole. I know she'll want in on this!*

She groaned when she turned the corner and saw the long line of people at all the checkouts. *Girl, you should've been paying better attention to the time. Oh well, maybe I will still be able to see five minutes of his practice.* When she entered the line, she never realized it would be her final choice of the day.

* * *

Lisa Fahrion scurried around, preparing the store for the busy day ahead. Back-to-school sales always meant the store would be hopping from the minute they opened to the minute they closed. Even though she knew her back and feet would be killing her at the end of the day, she was glad it would be busy because that meant the day would go by quickly. She planned to go by the animal shelter after work and help wash all the animals.

She had worked for Belk since she was a high school senior and worked her way to being an assistant manager. In her sophomore year of college, Lisa eagerly anticipated getting her degree and becoming a veterinarian. People always told her she could be a model since she was almost five foot six inches tall with long, wavy auburn hair, olive skin, and caramel-colored eyes, but she had grown up on a small farm and had always loved animals. She wanted to have her own clinic, but first, she had to finish school. Belk had been the only job she could find, and it helped pay her tuition. All her free time was spent volunteering at the local shelter.

The day was busier than expected, so she took a late lunch break. When she returned to the floor, one of the security guards approached her. "Miss, do you know where the store manager is? I need to speak with him."

"Well, he is out on vacation this week, so I'm acting manager until he gets back. What's going on?"

"Well, we have an emergency situation on our hands. I've already contacted emergency personnel, but you need to be aware that there is going to be an evacuation of the mall."

"An evacuation? Why? Did someone pull the fire alarm again?"

"We don't have time to get into it. Please! Immediately begin lockdown procedures and prepare for an evacu..." Before he could finish his sentence, the announcement came over the intercom telling shoppers to evacuate.

Chapter Six

"Calling all units! Calling all units! Code Orange at the Pilotview Mall. All officers report immediately." When he heard the dispatcher's words over his radio, fear gripped Curly's heart. Flipping on his sirens and lights, he turned his car around and prayed Shelly had already finished shopping. He again tried to reach her on his phone, but it went straight to voicemail.

He picked up his radio and called into the station to report his ETA, "Sheila, I will be there in ten minutes, but why is there a Code Orange? What's going on?" He weaved through the stopped vehicles and pressed down on the accelerator as far as it could go. He then swerved to avoid hitting a minivan that pulled out into the intersection.

"I don't know all the details. There was an explosion, maybe from a bomb," Sheila quickly replied

"What? A bomb? No way! Okay, my ETA is now five minutes, but Shelly was there shopping today, and I can't reach her. Hopefully, it's just because the towers are down, but could you put the word out and ask folks to keep an eye out for her?"

"Copy that." Throwing down the handheld mic, Curly tried to take deep breaths to dislodge the ball of dread in the pit of his stomach. *Come on, Lord, haven't we had enough? Please don't let anyone be hurt; please put your hand of protection around Shelly.*

* * *

Within seconds of the explosion, the wail of sirens echoed from every direction. Many of those who had been pulling out of the parking lot rushed back to help in whatever way they could while fully expecting to find no one alive after the magnitude of the blast. One of the volunteers, Bob Lancaster, an ER doctor, rushed to help whomever he could.

Realizing it would take the ambulances a few minutes to arrive, he went from victim to victim, looking for life. He had to constantly remind himself to shut out the horror taking place around him. The center of the store was now a huge hole. Anyone unfortunate enough to have been in the middle of the mall was just gone. Bob didn't think he would find anyone alive but was thankful to discover many of those on the fringe of the area hit were still struggling.

As the emergency personnel began arriving, he directed them to the worst cases. Unfortunately, many of the victims were either unconscious or dead and lacked identification, making the immediate task of determining their identities difficult. They just started loading victim after victim into the ambulances and sending them to the trauma unit at St. Joes' in nearby Winston-Salem.

Curly screeched to a halt at the parking lot's perimeter and was appalled at the scene before him. People were running, screaming, and crying. Bodies were lying everywhere. EMTs, police, and firemen from all surrounding counties were racing into the parking lot and going in every direction. He shook his head in disbelief. If he didn't know better, he would think he was on a movie set.

Oh my, Lord! This is worse than I had even expected. I hope Shelly has already left and is just trying to help people. Give me wisdom and strength, Lord.

Knowing it was up to him to get things organized, he gathered his emergency equipment and approached the scene, looking for where he wanted to start. Seeing a security officer kneeling by a bloody man on the ground, he asked, "Excuse me, I'm Lieutenant Greg Rogers. Do you know if anyone has begun to set up a command center anywhere?"

"Um, sir, I have no idea. I think everyone is just doing what they can until someone who knows what to do gets here," the officer answered as he continued to apply pressure to the man's shoulder.

"Okay, thanks. Keep it up!" Realizing he needed to start bringing some organization to the chaos, he directed the responding officers to help the worst victims. While he made his rounds through the chaotic scene, his mind kept going to his wife, wondering where she was and if she had found safety. Knowing he needed to concentrate on what was before him and help the public, he couldn't help but grow more and more concerned as he didn't find her among the living. So, as he worked on bringing some organization to the pandemonium, he pulled up a photo of her on his phone and started showing it to anyone he could. The churning in his stomach grew worse as time after time the person would just sadly shake their head. It was getting harder and harder to concentrate on giving orders and putting the public first. He was showing her photo to another security officer when his cell phone rang.

"Lieutenant Rogers here."

"Curly! A nurse over at St. Joes' just called. She thinks they have Shelly there!" Sheila was so excited that she screamed over the phone.

"Thinks? Why doesn't she know?" he demanded as he took off for his car.

"All she said is that the woman was unconscious with a huge gash on her head. She said she had seen the photo of you two in the paper after you got back from the cruise and thought this woman looked like her." Sheila quickly continued, "I've already contacted Tucker's school and am sending Chad to meet you there."

"Thanks, Sheila. Please tell Sergeant Richards to come to the mall's east side, where I have set up a command center. Once I hand over the command, I'll head over to the hospital to see if this woman is Shelly. Also, please update the chief that we have a huge mess on our hands, and I will return as soon as I make confirmation at the hospital." *Lord, if it is her, please let her live!*

Chapter Seven

Curly rushed into the ER, happy to see Tucker with his assistant coach, Coach Aram. Pulling him into a hug, he said, "Tuck! Boy, am I glad to see you. Have you seen your mama yet?"

"No, sir. We jest got here right 'fore ya walked in," he said trembling, while also trying to discreetly wipe the tears from his face.

"Come on then, let's go find her." As they turned to go to the reception desk, Aram turned to go with them. "Um, excuse me, Aram, maybe you best just wait here for us. I do appreciate you bringing him over from the school and waiting for me."

"Oh, excuse me, sir. I didn't think. I'm just as worried as you all are. Coach didn't want to just send him off with a police officer, and he went to help at the mall after getting Dave and Marc home. I told him I would be more than happy to accompany your boy."

"Okay, okay. I understand. His Uncle Chad should be arriving any minute. Right now, I need to see my wife. We'll talk to you in a little bit." As he and Tucker proceeded to the reception desk, Aram headed to the waiting room. At the desk, Curly explained the situation to a harried receptionist.

"I'm sorry. Let me call back into the ER and find out which patient they called you about." Before she could even punch in the numbers for the ER department, the phone started ringing, and more people started lining up, waiting to find out about their loved ones.

After ending that call, she looked at Curly, "Tell ya what—we have a mess on our hands. Since you're an officer of the law, I'm just gonna let ya go on back. Just ask the head nurse, Louise, when you get back there." She pushed the button to open the ER doors while turning to help the next one in line.

When Curly and Tucker entered the ER, they were immediately surrounded by mayhem. Emergency personnel raced from bed to bed, yelling orders as they went. The halls were lined with overflow patients, their beds crammed into every available space. Alarms and bells echoed nonstop.

With no head nurse—or any nurse, for that matter—at the station, Curly turned to Tucker. "Son, I'm gonna go find Shelly but I need you to wait right here 'til I do. You aren't allowed to be in these rooms." Noticing his wide eyes and pale face, Curly gave the boy's shoulder an encouraging squeeze before approaching the first bed.

Curly moved quickly, stepping behind each curtain, glancing at the patient, and then moving on to the next bed. He tried to stay out of the way, but the sight was disheartening—bed after bed brought only disappointment. Worse, he often caught a doctor or nurse pulling a sheet over a lifeless patient. He pressed on, grateful he'd told Tucker to wait in the hallway. At the tenth bed, he stepped behind the curtain and froze. Her beautiful hair confirmed it—he had found her.

Shelly! Please be okay! he prayed as he approached the bed.

"Officer, excuse us, but we need you to step out. You can question her once she's regained consciousness," a nurse reprimanded as she pointed him back out to the hallway.

"Ma'am, that is my wife, Shelly Gale Rogers. Please tell me she is going to be okay."

The doctor examining her looked up. "Well, at least we have a name for one patient now. At this moment, your wife is stable. She's unconscious and has a nasty head wound. Until I run some tests, I can't give a definitive prognosis."

The doctor finished taking her vitals. He then began to pull up her eyelids and shine a light in her eyes. As he continued the examination, he tried to reassure the worried husband, "I'll be ordering a full body MRI and blood work. I should have answers after reviewing her scans and blood work. Which could be a few hours. You are welcome to sit here and talk to her. She can probably hear you even though she may be unable to respond."

"Thank you, doctor. Let me get our boy back here, and I'll be glad to sit and talk to her all night."

"I'm sorry, but we only have space for one visitor. Either you or your son can stay with her. Although I will allow him to come in for just a minute to relieve his mind. If she remains stable, she'll be moved to the Neuro floor." At that, the doctor motioned for the nurse to follow him and hurried to the next bed, giving orders for Shelly's tests as he went.

Curly carefully brushed back the hair around her face, whispering, "We're just getting started, Shell—please stay with us. We need you. I love you!" He leaned over the railing, and after kissing her lips, he went to get Tucker.

Chapter Eight

Tucker waited for Curly to find his mom, blinking back tears that kept trying to escape. To distract himself, he watched the chaos unfold—doctors and nurses scrambling from bed to bed, desperately trying to help the endless stream of patients flooding into the ER. Ambulances arrived faster than anyone could manage, forcing many into the already full corridors. He wouldn't have thought anything would ever come close to the day he found his mom dead on their kitchen floor, but this scene was so horrific he kept catching himself thinking it had to be a TV show.

After enduring the groans and cries of the victims until he couldn't take it anymore, Tucker went to join Coach Aram in the waiting room. *Dad will come find me once he sees Mama Shelly. I just can't take any more of this. This is so unbelievable!*

When he entered the room, he was again overwhelmed by how crowded and loud it had gotten since they arrived. Obviously news had spread, and families were pouring in, desperate to find out if their loved ones had survived. He wished he were on *Star Trek*, able to teleport home and escape all the madness.

The crowded room made it hard to spot Coach Aram, so he looked for the bright yellow football sweatshirt the man always wore. After going through the waiting room and checking the snack area, he still could not find him. Thinking he had just missed him, Tucker searched the rooms again, asking if anyone had seen Aram. No luck.

Tucker finally figured his coach must be using the restroom and realized he needed to as well. He also wanted to wash off the grime from practice, as he felt like a smelly, dirty mess.

Not seeing his coach in the restroom, he shrugged and cleaned up the best he could. Upon leaving the restroom, he was relieved to see his Uncle Chad had arrived and was standing near the waiting room entrance. As he caught Chad up on all that had happened, he heard Curly's voice. "Tuck! Hey, Chad, am I glad to see you! This place is a zoo! I didn't see ya standing in the ER, so I figured you went to hang out with your coach." Looking around, he continued, "Where is he anyway?"

Tucker shrugged, "Don't ask me. I done looked through here twice and couldn't find him. Best I figure is he went on home. Who cares? I wanna go be with Mama Shelly. Is she okay? What is wrong with her? Is she gonna make it?" he asked.

Curly ran his hand through his curly brown hair, which had started to show a little gray. "She's alive, son. That's about all I can tell ya. Right now, she's not responding. The doc said I could take you back to see her, but then you'll have to go home or wait out here. Chad, wait here, and then take Tucker home?"

Having worked out the details with Chad, they turned a corner. Just two rooms down, Curly pulled back a curtain and motioned for him to enter.

She looked like she was sleeping, so Tucker reached out and touched her shoulder. "Hey, Mama Shelly, it's me, Tuck. Come on.

Wake up!" Not getting any response, he looked over to Curly, "She *is* going to wake up, right?"

Sighing, Curly ran his hands over his face, then held Shelly's hand. Struggling not to break down, he answered, "I pray so. The doctor is gonna need to run some tests before he can really tell us what to expect." As they stood by the bed, Curly wrapped his other arm around Tucker's shoulders and started quietly praying that whatever the doctor found would be minor and that she would wake up soon.

Watching Tucker reach out and touch her hand brought tears to his eyes. *Oh Lord, it's so hard seeing her like this, and Tucker has had more than his share of loss already in his short life. Please put your hand of protection and healing on her. Please, Lord.*

He ended the prayer and encouraged Tucker not to worry but to put her in God's capable hands. Several minutes later, a nurse pulled the curtain open and informed them it was time to take her for her MRI.

"I suggest ya'll go on out to the waiting room. We'll call ya'll when she's finished," Nurse Jenkins said while prepping Shelly's bed for transport.

"Okay. How long until we get the results? I really need to get back to the mall so I can get busy investigating this bombing, but I don't want to leave until we know what's wrong with her."

"It will be at least an hour and probably longer with so many to be examined. Why don't you go on ahead? We'll take good care of her, and I'll be glad to call you when we have the results. Just leave your cell number at the desk in the waiting room."

Frustrated between his desire to be with his wife and his duty as an officer, Curly reluctantly agreed, only after making the nurse promise to call with any updates. He then looked over at Tucker. "Okay. You and Chad head on home," he said. "Don't forget to feed Max and give him some fresh water. Chad, can you stay with him a while until I can get there?"

"Of course, Curly. Anything I can do to help. Wish I was already an officer so I could be helping at the mall. Don't worry about Tucker or Max; I have it all under control." Chad wrapped his arm around Tucker's neck and pulled him to give him a noogie.

"Thanks, man! That's a huge relief." *Wait. I completely forgot about Aram. Why would he leave like that? Strange.* Curly frowned. *I'll have to talk to him later. For now, I have much more serious things to figure out.*

They finally made their way through the mob of people and Curly found the car still at the curb where he had left it. As he got in the car, he took a few moments to answer texts. Knowing Nicole had started back to school, he called Tim and asked him to tell Nicole about Shelly. *Lord, please watch over her. I just found her and don't want to lose her. Please touch her and heal whatever is wrong, and I could sure use some wisdom and help in figurin' out who set that bomb off!*

Chapter Nine

Because Curly ran his lights and sirens, the trip across town to the mall only took a few minutes, despite the 5 o'clock rush hour. The whole way there, he struggled between his duty to the public and his duty as Shelly's husband. He felt guilty leaving her at the hospital. Shaking his head, he groaned, realizing he needed to call her parents.

Curly punched the speed dial number for the station precinct. "Sheila, I am on scene until I get word from the hospital. I need you to call Shelly's family in Ohio and let them know what's happened. I'll text you their number in a minute. Please tell them NOT to come down here right now and that I will call them tonight. Also, send an urgent message that all officers are to report to the command center here at the mall to receive their orders. It goes without saying that all vacation and leave time is on hold until further notice."

After texting Shelly's parents' phone number, Curly sat in the cruiser for a few moments, watching the unbelievable scene before him. Emergency personnel worked on the remaining casualties amongst the smoke from the burning building. All fire stations in the area had responded and were desperately trying to get the fire under control. They were a very well-organized machine and had made quite a bit of progress while he had been gone. He shook his head in disbelief, considering the huge task ahead for the crime scene crew.

Debris and bodies littered such a vast area that examining every part seemed nearly impossible. Sitting there thinking about it wasn't going to get anything done so Curly briskly walked toward the command center where a white canopy was set up on the outskirts of the parking lot. Usually, this area would be buzzing with loud, coarse officers cracking jokes. Today, however, everyone moved somberly through their duties, too overwhelmed to joke.

* * *

Nicole was interrupted from lesson planning by a knock on her classroom door and was pleasantly surprised to see it was her very handsome husband interrupting her. Rushing over, she opened the door. "Tim? What on earth are you doing here? Why aren't you at work?"

Tim grasped her hand, tugging her into a gentle hug.

"Tim! You're seriously scaring me here! What has gotten into you?"

"Nikki, babe. Man, I don't know how to say this, but you need to hear it straight from me. There's been an explosion at the Pilotview Mall. The news is reporting that there are many fatalities."

"Mall? What? I don't understand. A bomb at OUR mall? Wait! Shell was going there today. Oh no. Please, please tell me she's okay?" she begged as she tugged on his hands.

Pulling her close to him again, he continued, "She's alive but unresponsive at St. Joes' Hospital. Curly just called. It happened earlier today, but he just found her. He wants me to take you and Tucker back to the hospital to sit with her. Maybe by the time we get there, she'll be awake."

Stepping back, she quickly said, "Of course she will be! Just give me a second to get my stuff. But wait! I don't…"

Seeing she was working herself up into an anxiety attack, he quickly explained that he had already arranged with the principal for her to miss the next day or two. At that news, she rushed to her desk, got her things, and started filling her tote with textbooks. Just as she had gotten everything she would need, the principal walked through the door and assured her that all would be okay at school and that they were praying for Shelly. Hearing that, she ran out the door, urging Tim to hurry.

"Poor Tucker! He's already gone through so much. I'm sure he must be crazy with worry. Did they say if Shelly's going to make it? What's causing her to be in a coma?" Frustrated that Tim had no additional information, she leaned her head back on the car's headrest and started interceding with God on her best friend's behalf.

Chapter Ten

Since he had grown up in Pilotview, Curly knew most of the people he served. He appreciated living only four hours from the Atlantic Ocean while at the same time being only two hours from the Appalachian Mountains. Most days, he would arrive at work, grab a Coke Zero from his office refrigerator, and chat with Sheila about his family or her very spoiled and well-loved Maltese, Boo-Boo. After catching up with the others in the office, he would hand out assignments to his men before tackling any paperwork on his desk.

Pilotview had been a remarkably peaceful community where crimes rarely escalated beyond shoplifting or speeding. Since opioids, and especially heroin, had infiltrated his county, he found more and more of his time at the scenes of overdoses or arresting very young adults who were driving under heroin's influence. Each month, Curly and his pastor collaborated on a plan to help their beautiful town eradicate the drug and to help those currently enslaved to its horrific power.

He was very excited about his brother's upcoming graduation from the police academy and planned to hire him immediately. Eventually, he planned to assign Chad to lead a specialized team dedicated to tackling the opioid crisis, freeing up more time to deal with regular daily tasks like Jed's missing beef.

On the drive over to the mall, he had reminisced about the previous year when Tucker's biological dad had caused so much trouble. He and everyone else thought those events were the worst that their little town would ever see. Now, as he sat in his cruiser, trying to get the strength to open the door, he shook his head and wondered where to begin with the mess before him.

Reporters lined up along the road, parked as close to the yellow crime scene tape as possible. As Curly paused to talk to the officer guarding the entrance, they swarmed his car, shouting questions he couldn't answer—questions he doubted anyone but the bomber would know. After being waved through, he ignored the reporters and slowly found a parking spot. A couple of rookies stood in the command center, setting up a portable whiteboard while another officer printed mall and parking lot maps. He ordered one of them to locate any security officers, gather all the security footage, and load it onto the laptop. After getting that started, he had another officer start an ongoing list of known fatalities and another list of survivors with names and addresses.

Noticing several missed calls and voicemails from the mayor, he quickly called him and gave him an update on all they were doing. "Lieutenant Rogers, I need to hold a press conference as soon as possible. I'll tell them we'll hold it at six o'clock this evening there at the command center. That way, they can open their evening news with our updates. I expect you to be there to answer any questions that may arise. Meanwhile, I'm contacting the FBI to ask for their help. This is way beyond our capabilities and resources. Just keep me updated on any findings. Is that clear?"

Rubbing the back of his neck, Curly bit back a disgruntled sigh and answered, "Yes, sir. I will be here at the press conference. With respect, sir, I really don't like having the Feds messing with my case, but I completely understand and agree that we need them. How about giving us a week to investigate it ourselves first? Bring them in then if you still think they are needed at the end of the week."

After getting Mayor Carney's agreement, Curly disconnected the call and proceeded to take the mall map and draw lines on it to divide it up into sections. Each section was labeled, and he wrote the officers' names assigned to each section. Next, he texted the entire department, telling them to report to the center for their assignments. The first ones to arrive all inquired as to how Shelly was doing. He quickly realized he wasn't the only officer with a loved one at the hospital. It seemed every one of them had a friend or a relative who had been shopping that day.

Chapter Eleven

The week following the bombing was one of the most challenging, frustrating, and exhausting weeks of Curly's career. His days started with getting Tucker fed and off to school. Since he was the only parent at home, he was incredibly grateful they had switched to public school. At least now Tucker could take the bus, and he didn't have to drive him to school.

After making sure Tucker made it on time for the bus, he would clean up the kitchen and go for a run with Max. His runs were a vital part of his day. They helped clear his mind and he would spend the time pleading with God to heal his beautiful wife and help uncover the truth behind the bombing. Then it was to the hospital to check with the doctors and nurses on Shelly's condition.

After a week of little change, the doctors offered little hope that she'd come out of the coma. Curly could only place his trust in God that she would fully recover. He called her folks daily, giving them updates while encouraging them to stay in Ohio. He was thankful they decided not to come since Shelly's dad had an upcoming medical procedure himself, and Curly had no energy left to host them if they decided to visit.

After getting the doctors' updates, he would spend at least an hour sitting beside the bed, holding her hand, and talking to her. Early on, he'd decided to act like she could hear him and would wake up any minute, despite what the doctors said. So, he would pray aloud, read Scriptures, talk about Tucker's school life, and brainstorm about the case.

Then he would head to the station and try to keep up with the paperwork and any issues that came up. Since the bombing, they had not made any progress at all. All the lab reports came back stating that materials discovered were common, everyday items readily available in any American store. Despite the pages and pages of so-called witness phone calls, none were based in reality. He really didn't think an alien had planted a bomb. His favorite, though, was that an ISIS gang armed with assault rifles had been the ones to do it. *Like they would even have made it through the mall doors without security stopping them!*

With no progress to show, they finally decided to bring in the FBI for on-site assistance. The feds had been aware of the bombing and offering support in the background, but it was painfully clear that Curly needed them fully involved. He and his officers weren't exactly eager to work with the Feds, but at this point, they'd take any help they could get.

The FBI assigned two special agents, Agent Willis and Agent Tolley, to assist the Pioloview Police Department. Curly grew to appreciate and even respect both agents while working on the case. At first glance, Willis appeared to be a guy who would get run over in a confrontation. He was a single, six-foot-tall ginger covered with freckles and even had dimples when he smiled—being thin as a rail did not help make a strong impression either. But once he spoke, he had a way of taking immediate control with his deep voice. Exactly one week later, Curly realized Willis was quite fit despite his lankiness. He was able to hold his own with anyone.

On the other hand, Tolley couldn't be more different. He came across as everyone's favorite coach. A father of four, he knew how to be heard when needed. He was a large, physically fit man with arms that bulged every time he moved. Both men had worked as tirelessly as Curly and his officers, quickly earning the respect of the entire Pilotview Police Department.

Since it was essential to be there for Tucker, Curly was not about to complain about any extra help, especially with Shelly in the hospital. He was pulled in many different directions, making sure he picked Tucker up from practices and games, fed him, and ensured the boy completed his homework. They always made time to go sit with Shelly in the evening and update her on the day before heading home to start the whole exhausting process again the next day. Because he missed Shelly so much, he couldn't sleep very well, so he would spend his nights working on the case on his bed with the files spread out in front of him.

His church family wholeheartedly stepped up, offering as much help as possible. Thank goodness they were there, or Curly and Tucker would've been living on fast food. His Sunday school class organized a meal schedule so he wouldn't have to worry about preparing any dinners. Several members, including Nicole, offered to let Tucker stay with them or drive him to football practices and games.

As tempting as that was, Curly turned them all down. He knew his son was very worried about losing another mom, and he wanted to be the one to address any questions or concerns Tucker had. Curly knew it was hard enough for the boy to switch schools in eighth grade while adjusting to a whole new family, and now he had to worry about his mama on top of it. No, if he could manage it, he'd be the one taking care of his boy. He didn't adopt him for others to raise.

So here he was, a week after the worst crisis to happen in Pilotview, and no one had any idea how to find the perpetrator. As he and the agents sat in Curly's office, sifting through all the reports once again, he bit back a groan as he heard the unmistakable sound of Jed's voice coming down the hall. *Doesn't he realize we have a lot more important matters on our hands than a bunch of missing meat?*

Chapter Twelve

Tucker's week had been one of the longest of his life. He loved being able to go to the hospital with Curly, but at the same time, he dreaded it. He hated seeing his new mom lying in that hospital bed hooked up to all those noisy machines. It just wasn't fair that this was happening to him all over again. Every time he got to thinking about it, he would get so angry and would beg God to just let him be the next one to die. Life sucked anyway, so what's the point of living any longer if everyone he got close to was going to keep on dying?

Sometimes, late at night, he would get his phone out and start googling ways to commit suicide. He had worked out a plan, but he never could start putting it together because he was either at school or with Curly. After practices, Curly was always sitting right there in his squad car waiting for him so they could go to the hospital. He knew he should talk to someone about what he was feeling but had no idea how to even bring it up. He knew he should pray about how he felt, but he struggled to believe that God was truly there with him.

The only good parts of his days were when he was at football practices or roughhousing with their golden retriever, Max. Being on the football field was the only time of the day that he wasn't worried about Shelly dying. Besides, Coach Waddell and Coach

Aram were his two favorite people to be around. They were currently preparing the team for the regional conference that weekend.

At the start of the school year, all the middle schools in the area held a two-day tournament to give the teams some field time before the season began. The thought of it bummed him out—Tucker really wanted Mama Shelly in her usual seat, cheering him on. Maybe this weekend, during the tournament, he could find some alone time to start putting his plan into motion.

He was so ready for this practice to end. He had yet to do even one thing right, and he could tell his teammates and coaches were irritated with him. Never had he been so thankful to hear the coach's whistle signaling practice was over. Grabbing his stuff, he rushed toward the car so he wouldn't have to speak to anyone. He was also in a hurry to go and see Shelly.

"Hey, Tuck! Hold up! Tuck! Wait up, man!" he turned as he heard Aram yelling his name.

"What do ya need, Coach?" he asked as he continued walking to the parking lot.

"Just wondered how your mom is doing. She any better? Has she woken up yet?"

He hung his head and mumbled, "I don't know why you even care after leaving me at the hospital like that, but, no, she's not any better and is still in a coma. Doctors are saying she will probably never come out of it." Coach Waddell joined them as they got to the edge of the parking lot. He had overheard Tucker's answer, so he slung his arm around the boy's shoulders.

"Hey, man, I know you have a ton of stuff on your mind right now, so don't let this practice get you down. You're still one of my best running backs, and we're all pulling for your mom to get better. Don't let life knock you off your feet, either. Is there anything we can do for ya?"

"Nah, I don't reckon there is," Tucker mumbled as he stood there with his hands in his pockets and head hanging down.

"Well, if you ever want to talk or just hang out with this old man, just give me a holler. Any time! I mean it! I'm here for you!" Coach Waddell slapped him on the back while sharing a concerned look with Aram.

Aram cleared his throat and tried again to get him to talk. "Listen, Tuck, I know you are upset with me about not hanging around in the waiting room. I should've told you my sister had texted me needing a ride. A bunch of us are going to Pizza World around six thirty, and after that, we're heading to the movies to see an action movie that just came out. If you want to join us, shoot me a text, and I'll come pick you up. Several of the guys are hoping you will come. They specifically asked me to invite you."

Tucker shrugged. "I doubt it. I'll ask Curly, but we've been sticking at the hospital till late, and I want to be there with Mama Shelly. If I decide to go, I'll text ya. See ya!" He turned, jogged toward the waiting car, threw his bags in the back seat, and slammed the passenger door. "Let's get out of here!"

Curly looked over in surprise at the slammed door and asked "I take it something happened at practice?" When he only got a shrug for an answer, he pulled out into traffic and turned in the direction of the hospital. "Well, if you need to talk, I'm always here for you." Tucker kept his gaze out the passenger window so Curly continued, "I'm having trouble myself. I'm so worried about Shelly, and on top of that, I have this bombing to figure out. Then, this afternoon, I got a call from my mom saying my dad had been admitted to Hospice. I'm trying hard not to worry and let God handle it, but it seems as soon as I finish praying about it, I catch myself worrying about it all over again." He reached over and squeezed Tucker's shoulder. "Son, I know this isn't easy for you either. I just want to help you if I can." When he noticed Tucker discreetly trying to wipe the tears off his face, he decided to just shut up and give the boy some space.

As they walked into Shelly's room, Curly was glad to see Nicole and Tim were already in Shelly's room. "Hey, ya'll! It's sure good to see you!" He reached out and gave Nicole a quick hug and then shook Tim's hand.

"Good to see you two as well, but I have to say, you look like something my barn cat has dragged in and stomped on. Land's sakes, Curly! Look at those black bags under your eyes! Do ya think Shell is gonna want to wake up and stay awake if she sees you looking like that? And, Tuck, honey, what's wrong? What's been making you cry?" Not waiting for any answers, she pulled Tucker into a huge hug and rubbed his back. "Listen, none of this mopey face business, ya hear me?" She stepped back while keeping both hands on his shoulders and looked him in the eye. "Your Mama is gonna wake up anytime now. Why we've got a group on Facebook with over two thousand folks already in it and all of them promising to pray and have their churches pray! So you just wipe those tears away and come tell me and Tim all about yer upcoming tournament this weekend. Who is it ya'll are playing again? And what time do we need to be there?"

She pulled him over to the window and wrapped her arm around him, determined to get a smile out of him before they left. Curly quietly released a huge sigh of relief and took up his vigil by his wife's bed. He grabbed her hand as he started praying. *Lord, I need your help. I know nothing about raising kids, especially a young and grieving teen. I'm clueless on how to help him with this, and Shelly would be so good at it. Please let Nicole or someone reach him and help him with all this. And I know I've already asked a zillion times, but it sure would be nice if you would let her wake up.*

Chapter Thirteen

After he finished praying, Curly tuned in to the conversation going on between Tucker and Nicole, noting she wasn't getting much out of him either. He missed his son's usual talkative and outgoing spirit. Right now, he would even take some of his quick sarcasm, but that had been missing all week as well. Sitting there holding Shelly's hand, unsure how to help Tucker when he couldn't even see a way through this himself, he heard a loud argument escalating in the hallway. He motioned for everyone to stay put and stepped out to see what was causing all the ruckus.

He came to a sudden stop and groaned when he saw Nate Atkins, his least favorite reporter with WPIL, at the nurses' station, loudly demanding to see the Lieutenant. Hearing Curly's groan, Nate glanced in the officer's direction and quickly called out, "Lieutenant Rogers! There you are! I must speak with you immediately, but this woman here won't let me through!"

Not giving the man an opportunity to continue, Curly immediately held up his hand, "Stop! I can't believe you would stoop so low as to barge in on our family when we're so worried about Shelly. You've been given all the updates you are going to get from the press conferences. Now leave before I have this lovely nurse get security to escort you out of here."

Nate ran over and grabbed Curly's arm before he turned back into the room. "Hold up, man! I'm not here for information! Well, unless you want to give me some. I'm here because our station has received a letter from the bomber. It was hand-delivered today. My boss called the station looking for you and when he heard you were here at the hospital, he sent me to get you. You have got to see this for yourself, sir. It's not good."

"First, get your hand off me immediately, and don't ever grab any officer's arm like that again if you value your life. Second, tell me, why should I believe you? Ya'll are always coming up with ways to get me over there so you can spring an interview with me. Nate, I have way too much to deal with to be playing these games today."

Nate instantly removed his hand from Curly's arm, held his hands up in the air to calm Curly down, and then sighed as he stepped back. "I know! I know! You're exactly right! We have been guilty of doing that a few times in the past; however, I'm not making this up! It's serious, Lieutenant, extremely serious. He or she demands we read their included statement tonight on the eleven o'clock news."

Curly took a moment to look Nate over and realized he looked like he had jumped up and run out of his office in the middle of something. In all the time Curly had known him, the man always looked camera-ready, with perfect jet-black hair and tailored suits matched with coordinating ties. Today, however, no jacket, sleeves rolled up, hair mussed as if he had been running his hands through it—he looked nothing short of rattled.

"Okay, Nate, I'm probably a fool, but I think you might be

telling me the truth, mainly because you look like a train wreck. But I'm warning ya, if you're lying to me…"

"No, no! I'm not! Come on, man, we don't have much time!"

Curly signaled Nate to wait when the man started toward the elevators. Then he stepped into Shelly's room, confirming with Tim and Nicole that Tucker could stay with them for the evening. After he had Tucker taken care of, he reached down and gave Shelly a quick kiss on the cheek, and headed out to see what had their local reporter so stressed.

After Curly left, Tucker turned to Nicole and Tim, "I jest want some time alone with my mama. Do ya'll think that'd be ok?"

Nicole pulled him into another hug, fighting back another round of tears. "Of course! That's a wonderful idea. Tim and I will just head on down to the cafeteria. I have a mighty hankering for some coffee and cake. You text us if you need something, okay?" At Tucker's nod of agreement, Nicole and Tim exited the room.

Tucker settled into the chair next to his mother's bed, clasping her hand in both of his. *God, I jest can't take much more of this. What have I done to deserve losing ANOTHER mama? And Mama Shelly is the nicest, sweetest woman on the face of the whole earth. She surely hasn't done nothin' to deserve this. What am I gonna do without her?*

The television station buzzed with activity, people rushing everywhere and phones ringing nonstop. Curly couldn't fathom how on earth anyone could get anything accomplished with all the noise. He followed Nate through a twisting maze of cubicles to a group of offices at the back of the room. Nate opened a door labeled "Conference Room C" and motioned for Curly to take a seat.

"I need to grab my boss and the letter," Nate said. "I'll just be a minute. If you want some coffee, help yourself." He gestured at the machine in the back corner. "It's all right there. I'll be back shortly."

A couple of minutes later, Nate returned with an older, gray-haired man dressed in a charcoal three-piece suit who was holding a large Ziploc bag that looked like it had a brown envelope inside.

"Lieutenant, thank you for coming so quickly. I'm Larry Boreo, the owner. Didn't Nate get you some coffee?"

"No, thank you. I just want to see what ya'll got today."

Larry placed the bag on the large conference table and pushed it over to him. "This arrived an hour ago. It was hand-delivered to Mr. Atkins by an older teen girl. Not realizing the importance of the contents, Mr. Atkins didn't think to inquire as to why she was hand-delivering mail. As soon as he read it, he brought it to my attention. I believe you know the rest. Now, I'll hush so you can see for yourself why we're so concerned."

Curly reached into his coat pocket and removed the latex gloves he always carried. After putting them on, he carefully opened the bag and pulled out a six-by-nine plain brown envelope that had WPIL in black, block letters printed on the front. He gently pulled the enclosed sheet of plain white copy paper out and started to read:

We demand the following statement be read on the 11 o'clock news tonight, or you will lose someone close to you:

"To the people of Pilotview,

No one is safe in this town. The mall bombing was just a speck of dust compared to the destruction you will see in the coming weeks. If you wish to put a stop to this, we must receive 5 million dollars. Tell Lieutenant Rogers we will contact him tomorrow, Tuesday, August 28th, at 9 pm with his instructions. If this amount is not paid on time, no one will be safe."

~ The Omega

Chapter Fourteen

With only hours to put a plan in place, Curly decided to call in the big guns. He quickly sent a group text to Agents Willis and Tolley detailing the situation and asking them to meet him at the television station for a strategy session. While waiting for them to arrive, he reviewed the station's security footage, searching for clues that would point them in the right direction so they could avoid dealing with the demands. However, it was precisely as Nate described: a teenage girl dressed in shorts and a tank top approached the receptionist, asked for someone, and then Nate approached and briefly talked with the girl for a few seconds, before taking the envelope.

He watched until the girl left, and then Nate strolled back to his cubicle. Nothing was on the tapes at all to help. The girl looked like any other girl her age, but he still needed to locate her to find out who had paid her for the delivery. By the time he finished reviewing the feed, the agents had arrived.

The owner graciously allowed them to continue using the same room. Before they started, Curly turned to Nate. "Hey, do ya'll have any soda machines? I could really use a Coke Zero."

"Sure. In fact, we even have a Coke machine. Just have a seat; I'll be glad to get it for ya. Agents, would ya'll like one as well?" The agents pointed to the coffee they had just poured, so Nate left to get Curly his drink.

Once he had exited the room, Curly turned to the agents and said, "He won't be gone long, so we need to hurry. Quickly read this, and then we'll discuss whether our helpful reporter is behind all of this." Curly pushed a copy of the letter between them.

Seeing it was just a copy, Willis looked up and asked, "Hey! What's this? Where's the original?"

"I have it sealed in an evidence bag which makes it harder to read. Quick, just read it."

A few minutes later, Tolley leaned back, running his hands over his face. "Great! As if dealing with a bomb scene wasn't enough, we now must worry about a ransom!"

Willis nodded in agreement while looking intently at Curly. "I don't think we can definitively say that Mr. Atkins is our guy just from this," he said. "Still, we should keep him at the top of our suspect list. I see him heading our way, so let's move on to how to deal with this demand."

Nate walked in, handed Curly his soda, and pulled out a chair. Before he was seated, Agent Willis held up his hand, "Wait! What do you think you are doing?"

Nate stepped back and looked around in confusion. He replied slowly, "Who me? I'm just going to sit down."

"No, you aren't. You are a civilian. As such, you cannot be a part of this discussion. While we appreciate you bringing this to our attention so quickly, I must now insist you leave. We will call for you when we have decided on the best way to proceed." Willis raised his eyebrows when Nate didn't move. "In case you didn't understand what I just said, go!"

"Since I'll be the one reading this on the air tonight in just a couple more hours, I have every right to be here."

"No, you have zero right to be here. In fact, if you don't leave in the next thirty seconds, I will have you arrested for obstruction of justice." Willis pointedly looked at his watch.

Realizing the agent was serious, Nate harrumphed and slammed the door on his way out. Once he left, Curly turned back to the agents. "Well, I'd say that's putting yourself smack in the middle of this investigation. And Nate Atkins just jumped to the top of my suspect list. Now, what are we going to do about these demands? Do we ignore his request to read this on the air? If we allow him to read this, it will cause even more panic, not to mention Pilotview doesn't have five million dollars."

Willis motioned for Tolley to respond, "Lieutenant, no, we aren't going to allow a criminal to dictate what we do." Seeing Curly shaking his head in protest, he held up his hand and added, "We're going to write a letter back to *The Omega* and have Nate read it on air tonight."

"What? Are ya'll nuts?"

Willis responded, "Well, Tolley probably is nuts, but his plan is the best way to handle this problem. Let's get busy working on the wording of our response."

Curly lowered his head into his hands and shot a quick prayer for help. *Oh, Lord, help. I don't want anyone else to die, and these two are going to get more people killed playing these games.*

Chapter Fifteen

"Okay. Let's take a breath and figure out how we're going to handle this," Agent Willis said snapping a photo of Omega's note with his phone. "Whoever sent this has already waited over a week. This tells me he's seeking attention from the media and isn't happy with our lack of progress. If he had truly done this only for money, he wouldn't have waited this long to make his demands." Hearing Curly's phone start ringing, he paused in his profile.

Seeing it was Nicole calling, Curly stood and started towards the door to get some privacy. "Excuse me a minute; I have to take this." He stepped out into the hallway as he hit the answer option on the screen. "Hey, what's up, Nicole?"

"You gotta get back over here to the hospital as quickly as you can. The doctors need to talk to you. We tried to find out what's going on, but they said that they can only talk to you. Something's going on, so get here quick!"

"I'm at WPIL, so I'll be there in ten minutes. Tell the doctor to call my cell if he needs something before I see him." Putting his phone in his back pocket, Curly rushed back into the conference room to inform the agents that he had to leave right away. After agreeing to meet with them later, once he had news about Shelly, he anxiously dashed out, desperate to get to his wife.

As he rushed down the hospital corridors heading towards

Shelly's room, he grew alarmed by the crowd of nurses, doctors, and friends standing outside the door of her room. Curly barely noticed Nicole, Coach Aram and his wife, Lisa, standing there as he pushed into the room. Just as he pushed the door open, his eyes locked with Tucker's, and he saw the terror in his son's eyes. He gripped Tucker's shoulders and quickly said, "Son, I'll let you know as soon as I know something. Just pray,"

"Dr. Catania, what's going on here? What has happened? Is Shelly okay?" he demanded as the doctor bent over her bed.

"There you are. Mrs. Sheldon said you would be here quickly, and she was right. Could everyone please give us the room?' After everyone had vacated, the doctor shut the door.

Curly's heart raced as he tried to refrain from yelling. "Doctor, please tell me what is going on with Shelly."

The doctor sighed, rubbed his hands over his face. "From what I understand, Mr. and Mrs. Sheldon had taken your son, Tucker, to the cafeteria to grab some dinner. While they were gone, Mrs. Roger's oxygen levels dropped drastically, which set off the alarm. Fortunately, a nurse heard it and rushed in to find that her oxygen tube was lying on the floor."

"What? How did that happen?"

The doctor spread his hands in hopelessness. "We're in the process of looking into it, but I have some good news for you. While examining her just now, she opened her eyes a couple of times and gripped my hand when I requested her to."

Hearing that his wife had responded to the doctor's commands, Curly rushed over to her bed. He grabbed her hand and started rubbing the back of it while whispering, "Come on, honey, please open your eyes for me. It's Curly. I love you and miss you so much. Tucker and I both need you so very much. Please wake up for me."

He struggled not to start crying while anxiously waiting to see if she would respond. After a few seconds, she turned her head and blinked while squeezing his hand. "There you are! Oh, Shell! We've missed you so much! Welcome back!" He leaned over and gave her a big kiss. "Doctor, would you mind letting her friends out in the hallway know that they can come back in so they can see the good news?"

"Um, wow! What on earth is going on? Why are you crying?" She winced as she coughed to clear her throat. After licking her dry lips, she continued, "And, before you answer that, could you please get me something to drink?" Her face twisting from being so weak, Shelly struggled to sit up in the bed.

"Honey, please just lie still. You need to take it easy. Here, drink some water." Curly held the cup of water to her mouth while she sipped from the straw. When she finished, he handed her his lip balm to help her chapped lips. "You were shopping at Belk, and someone set off a bomb in the mall. We're so very thankful that you survived and that you're awake now."

"A bomb? In the mall? I want to hear more about this, but first, I need to see Tuck."

Curly shook his head, "Shelly, honey, you need to rest. Just lie there and sleep. You can see everyone later."

"No, I must see him. Then I will nap. I promise."

"Okay, but just for a minute or two. I'll be right back." Curly turned and motioned for Tucker to come on in to the room from the doorway where he hesitantly stood with Nicole and Tim.

Tim and Nicole stepped back as Curly nudged Tucker over to her bed. Seeing that his mom was truly awake and talking, he leaned over and placed a kiss on her cheek. "Mama Shell, ya scared us real bad. I can't have no more parents a dyin' on me! And I did jest like ya taught me though, and prayed all day every day that God would let ya wake up. I can't believe it, but He answered my prayers!"

Seeing how emotional he was, she grabbed both his hands and said, "Nah, God has more for me to do here on this earth, including being your mama for a lot longer." Before she could continue, Nicole came up next to Tucker and leaned down to give her best friend a long hug.

"Shell! Boy are we glad to see you awake and talking!" Nicole said as tears streaked her face. "I can't even begin to tell you how scared we've been that we would never hear your voice again. You and I have loads to catch up on, but for now, you just need to spend some time with your fellas, so Tim and I are gonna skedaddle out of here. We're gonna swing by your place and check in on Max. I will come back in a couple of hours with some of your clothes and your favorites from Chick-fil-A." After writing down a list of specific things Shelly wanted from her apartment, Nicole and Tim said their good-byes and left.

"Okay, you two, sit down right here next to me and tell me what on earth happened. A bomb? I just can't wrap my mind around a bomb at the mall! Who on earth would do such a thing?"

Chapter Sixteen

Curly entered the police station to find Willis and Tolley working away in the conference room with all of his officers, hoping they had prepared a statement for Omega. Needing quiet to gather his thoughts, he retreated to his office so he could just think and draw up one of his lists. Sitting down at his old, scarred, cluttered desk, he grabbed a notecard and started listing ideas bubbling in his brain.

1 - Who delivered the letter to WPIL

2 - Get Chad to canvas Jed's neighborhood for anyone suspicious

3 - Meet new resident that Pastor Thomas had mentioned, retired state trooper Alan

4 - Review all cell phone photos and videos from right before bomb went off

5 - Set up a tip line

6 - Don't forget to get Chad a graduation gift for graduation - one week

Before he could think of anything else to add, his cell started ringing. Seeing it was his new father-in-law, he grinned and leaned back in his chair as he answered, "Hey, Roger! Have you heard the great news about your baby girl?" After catching him up to date, he then spent several minutes encouraging him to stay at home and not come for a visit. "Roger, honestly, right now isn't a good time. Between you just having that procedure on your knee and me being swamped at work, I just don't think we can do it. I know how badly you want to be here. How about you call every day and if she gets worse then you can fly down? Otherwise, let's plan something in a month or so."

It took several minutes to wind down the call, and once it ended, he immediately called Chad to get him started canvassing Jed's neighborhood. They needed to see if they could track down the meat thief since all his paid officers were currently assigned to the bombing investigation. Having taken care of Jed, Curly grabbed a Coke Zero from his mini-fridge and made his way to the conference room.

Willis and Tolley sat at the end of a large table glued to their tablets while several officers sifted through papers.

"Hey, ya'll, I have some fantastic news! Shelly is awake and talking! And that's about all I know at this point. We're waiting to hear if the doc is gonna let her go home tomorrow."

He paused as everyone cheered and clapped, then he rubbed his hands together and looked straight at the two Feds as he continued, "Now, where are we? Someone catch me up and give me something to focus on other than Shelly."

Willis took the lead and explained that the officers were reviewing statements from the day of the bombing and were running background checks on all survivors. He and Tolley were finalizing the statement for Omega, recommending either the Mayor or Curly read it at a press conference. After being briefed, Curly offered to schedule the conference and said he would also announce a tip line for anyone with information regarding that day.

"So, Willis, after I get that taken care of, I think my time would best be spent studying the security tape from WPIL, and hopefully, I'll find a still shot good enough to release to the public at the press conference."

"Hey! Great idea! We are about finished here, and next, we will see what your officers have found in the background checks of the mall personnel and our annoying reporter, Nate, from WPIL."

"Sounds great. Keep me posted." Curly looked around and was glad to see one of his sharpest officers, Nick Vincent, was working and following their conversation. "Hey, Nick, I could use your help and eyes on this video. Meet me in my office in twenty minutes, and we'll see if we can force a break in this case." After getting Nick's nod of agreement, Curly set off back to his office to get the press conference set up.

* * *

Everyone except Tucker had finally left the hospital, and Shelly was enjoying having him nearby, playing on his phone while she dozed off and on. Seeing she was awake, Tucker started telling her about his tournament that weekend and how he did not think they stood a chance. He then told her that his coach had given them all a big, boring talk about how even though they didn't know if they would win, they still had to play their best and might even place second or third.

"Oh, Mama Shell! I 'bout plumb forgot to tell you what Pastor Thomas told me! 'Member how the youth group is going to South Africa next month to help our missionaries, the Simmons, with Vacation Bible School? Well, Pastor told me Sunday night after youth group that someone had paid for me to go too! Can you believe it? I didn't think I could go with ya bein' so sick and all but now you're awake and…" Tucker gave her a big grin and shrugged his shoulders.

Shelly laughed and grabbed his hand to pull him over to the bed. "Why don't you lie down here next to me so I can mess your hair up?" After he had gotten settled, she ran her fingers through his thick red hair as she answered, "That's awfully generous of someone. It would be a wonderful experience for you for sure, but I don't know how I feel about you being on the other side of the world and your dad and I here. Let me pray about it, then run it by Curly to see what he thinks. We also need to discuss it with Pastor. Hey! Maybe they could use another chaperone. I would love to see Beth and Mark and their two kids and spend some time with them. When did Pastor say he needed an answer?"

Tucker shrugged while mumbling, "I can't 'member 'cause I didn't think I could go. Man, I'll have to see if Marc and Dave are going too. South Africa! Wow! Maybe we will see a lion!"

Shelly chuckled and closed her eyes as the drowsiness returned. *Lord, what a wonderful gift someone gave him and us. Please give Curly and me wisdom on how to proceed. And help Curly find the person responsible for the horrific bombing.*

Chapter Seventeen

Knowing every news organization within driving distance would show up for this press conference, Curly was thankful they had a Carolina blue sky day as the conference was set up on the front steps of City Hall to allow for the expected large numbers. Despite the mayor demanding to hold it the night before, he had relented to the agent's insistence to wait until morning. The mayor hadn't liked it but wouldn't argue with the agents. Having the conference at ten o'clock meant it would still make the noon newscast. Seeing all was ready and everyone who was speaking was on stage, Curly gave Mayor Carney's assistant, Lucas, the nod to begin.

Lucas didn't look very intimidating at five-foot-eight inches tall. He was a wiry black man, but because of his extra deep, gruff voice he could instantly bring large crowds under control within seconds. As usual, as he introduced the press conference, everyone stopped talking and settled down.

"Ladies and gentlemen, please quiet down. Mayor Carney will speak first, followed by Special Agent Willis and then Lieutenant Rogers, in that order. Mayor Carney will add a few remarks at the end before opening it up to your questions. Now, please welcome Mayor Carney." He stepped aside and motioned with his hand toward the mayor as everyone clapped.

Curly and his captain stood at attention as the mayor went on and on in his usual style about how the city's safety was their number one concern and how all their manpower was being implemented to bring those responsible to justice, blah, blah, blah. As he kept rambling on, Curly had to bite his lip to stop a grin when he spotted his brother, Chad, on the perimeter of the crowd, rolling his eyes when he caught Curly's attention. *Thanks, Chad, trying to get me to slip up, as always.*

He scanned the crowd, looking for anyone who stood out. He wished Shelly and Tucker could've been there but was thankful the doctor had discharged her early that morning. She was currently resting at home watching the press conference with Tucker. He also had to send a quick prayer of thanks that Tucker was responsible enough to stay home from school to help her while he was busy working. *Of course, don't know too many teens who wouldn't mind missing school to sit at home on their phones playing games.* Finally, he heard the mayor turn the podium over to Agent Willis.

Willis confidently strode to the podium, adjusted the microphone higher since he was several inches taller than the mayor, and began his prepared statement.

"As you heard on WPIL last night, we have been contacted by a group called 'The Omega.' We have developed a profile and have distributed it to all the various police agencies. While we will not give you the entire profile, we do want the public to know that the leader of this group is a white, single male between the ages of twenty and thirty. He is unemployed and lives at home with his parents. He blends in because he is of average build and is a very quiet person that people just don't seem to notice. Regarding the demands in Omega's letter, as we said in our response last night, we do not and will not give any money to any terrorists. What Omega did at your mall is an act of terrorism. Thank you. That's all I have for today." As he stepped back to his spot on the stage, the reporters erupted in shouts of questions.

After Willis returned to his spot, Curly stepped up to the podium and stood there staring straight ahead, not saying a word until the crowd finally realized he would not speak until they were quiet. Once they had settled down again, he cleared his throat and began:

"We at the Pilotview Police Department are working hand-in-hand with Special Agent Willis and Special Agent Tolley. We are following several leads and promise you that we are giving this our full focus. This was an act of cowardice and the man or men responsible are using this group Omega to hide behind. We will not stop until we have arrested every person responsible. We ask the wonderful citizens of Pilotview to help us by reporting anything you see or hear that is suspicious. A tip line has been set up for you to contact us regarding any suspicious activity. You can text us at the Pilotview police station at #PTVW or call 888-555-PTVW. This information is also available on our website and our Facebook page. Thank you, and now I will turn it back over to Mayor Carney to wrap things up."

Back in their apartment, Shelly pulled her cell phone out and texted Curly,

> Great job! Just wish I could've seen your curly hair better! You were very official-looking and did an outstanding job. Loves ya!

She looked over at Tucker and said, "Your dad was on television! You'll be famous at school now."

"Ha ha! More like the guys will give me a hard time over it. Ya doin' okay? Need anythin'?"

She smiled while rubbing Max's head, who was snuggled up to her as close as he could get. "You are such a sweetie and doing such a good job taking care of me that I don't need a thing. I'm just going to keep snuggling Max while lying here catching up with everyone on Facebook." Hearing his name, Max stretched out his front paw and put it on her shoulder. "Oh, Nicole just texted me and said she and Tim are going to come by after work tonight. She's bringing her famous lasagna and some sweet tea."

Tucker threw both arms up in the air and yelled, "Yes! I love that lasagna of hers. Was really 'fraid we would be stuck eating cereal again since Curly is gonna be busy tonight."

"That he is. Hey, since the press conference is over, why don't you and I take Max for a very short walk, and you can toss him the Frisbee for a bit? I could use some fresh air after being cooped up in that hospital." As he helped her get her tennis shoes on and the leash on Max, Shelly took a moment to shoot a quick prayer for Curly. *Lord, he just put himself front and center for this madman. Please keep him safe and give him direction so he can nail this guy.*

As she and Tucker opened the front door, they heard a reporter interrupt *The Price is Right* with a breaking news logo flashing across the television. "This just in. A bomb just went off on the stage while Mayor Carney was answering questions at the press conference. We have not been informed if the mayor survived or not."

Shelly froze as terror gripped her heart. Another bomb? At the press conference? The one Curly was at? *Oh no, Lord, please no!*

Chapter Eighteen

Shelly frantically handed Max's leash to Tucker and called Curly on his cell phone. When it went straight to voicemail, she groaned and sent him a quick text. "Tuck, we aren't waiting for him to reply. I need to know if he's okay or not, so take Max out front, and when he's done with his business, load him up in the car. I'm going to grab my pocketbook and lock up the apartment. We're going to find him, and there's no telling how long that will take." *Lord, please, please, please let him be okay. I pray no one was hurt but please let him be okay. Ugh, WHY hasn't he answered yet?* She quickly gathered her things, locked the apartment, and ran to the car, glad to see Tucker and Max were already waiting for her.

Just as she opened her door, she heard her neighbor girl, Brittany, call out, "Hey, Miss Shelly, is everything ok?" from her front porch.

Shelly quickly replied, "Yes!" then jumped into the car before anyone else could delay her.

Seeing Tucker's pale face, she reached over and grabbed his hand. "I know, honey, I know. I'm worried too, but while I drive, you just keep praying and trusting God. Until we know for sure otherwise, he's okay."

Thankfully, traffic was light as she raced over to City Hall. Once she was closer, traffic came to a complete stop due to all the emergency vehicles. Growing frustrated and almost sick with worry, she managed to get her car to the Starbucks' parking lot and parked her car. "Come on, fellas, let's go find Curly. He's got to be somewhere in the middle of this madness." She took off at a jog, looking in every direction while hoping to see her tall, handsome husband. *Please, Lord, please let me find him, and let him be ok.*

The scene around City Hall was complete pandemonium. Police had strung yellow tape to keep everyone from getting too close, but people were jostling and pushing, trying to get as close as they could to see the devastation. Sirens wailed, voices screamed, and officers shouted for people to stay back. Spotting Curly's favorite officer, Nick, standing guard, she pushed her way up to him and yelled, "Nick! Where's Lieutenant Rogers? I can't reach him. Please tell me he's okay!"

"Mrs. Rogers? What are you doing here? Come on," he said, lifting the tape and motioning her to the other side as he continued, "One of the paramedics told me he had heard the Lieutenant was hurt, but I don't know how badly or where he is. Let me see if I can get someone to help you, 'cause I can't leave my post, or these people will swarm worse than ants on honey."

As Nick used his shoulder radio to find some help for her, Shelly heard the most beautiful sound she had ever heard in her life—Curly shouting that he wasn't going to the hospital.

"Tuck! Do you see him? I just heard him!"

Suddenly, Max yipped and took off running, dragging Tucker behind him. Shrugging, Shelly followed as Max weaved past several officers and ambulances. The dog skidded to a stop and leaped onto Curly, who was sitting on the edge of a gurney behind one of the ambulances. A paramedic stood next to him with his hands on his hips.

"Max? Tucker? What on earth are you two doing here?" Laughing as Max put his paws on Curly's knees and yipped at him, Curly rubbed his head and continued, "Yeah, yeah, love you too, big boy, but stop it. Enough!" As soon as he had Max pushed down and sitting, Shelly had arrived. She and Tucker both launched themselves into his arms. "Hey! Not that I'm complaining, but what's this? I'm fine. I'm okay. Shell, honey, why are ya'll even here?"

"Oh, Curly, I can't even tell you how relieved I am to see you and hear your voice. We had the tv on, and they interrupted *Price is Right* with breaking news. They said a bomb had gone off and that they didn't know if anyone had been hurt or killed. Knowing you were one of the speakers, I've been a basket case thinking you had been hurt or even worse."

"Why didn't you just call or text?" he asked reaching for his cell phone. His face fell when he saw it in pieces. "Oh, guess the blast took care of that. Looks like I'll be getting a new phone. Okay. Well, as you can see, I'm quite all right."

At the paramedic's harrumph, Curly shrugged sheepishly, "Well, mostly okay. The mayor was winding things down, so I'd already started to exit the stage when the blast happened. If it had been even just a couple of seconds earlier, I would be with Jesus right now. I just got knocked down and all kinds of debris hit me in the back. The paramedics and I were just discussing whether I should go to the hospital or not. I'm fine and I need to be here to look after things."

Putting her hands on either side of his face, she leaned over and rested her forehead on his. "Honey, please listen to them. I am so very thankful you feel good enough to argue with them, but Tuck and I need you to be okay. Now, you *are* going to let them take you to be checked out. I will get Chad to meet me at the ER so he can take Tuck and Max back home. I'm sure your brother is as worried about you as I was."

"Chad? Oh, he's here somewhere in this madhouse. He was at the press conference rolling his eyes at me. Shell, I can't leave. The blast took out my chief and the mayor both. Someone needs to be in charge, and that would be me.

As Shelly continued to reason with him to take care of himself, Agents Willis and Tolley rushed over. Willis reached his hand out and rested it on Curly's shoulder.

"You are a sight for very sore eyes. Listen to your wife, Lieutenant. Tolley and I will handle things here and will stop by the hospital after we have the crime scene secured and the techs busy collecting evidence. Now, don't worry about any of this. We have it under control. Go on to the hospital and take care of yourself."

Realizing he was outnumbered and out-maneuvered, Curly allowed the paramedic to insert the IV and load him into the ambulance. As the doors shut, Shelly called out, "Love you, honey. I'll be right behind you!" Once they had pulled away, she called Chad and filled him in on what was going on with Curly. As they talked, he wound his way through the crowds toward them.

"There ya'll are! Shell! Are you positive Curly is okay? I started looking for him but kept getting stopped to help people who were hurt," he said as he pulled her into a hug.

"He was good enough to argue with everyone about going to the hospital. You know him; he was determined to stay here to make sure everything got done right. Look, can you run Tuck and Max home for me and bring Curly some regular clothes to the hospital? He was still in his dress uniform."

After working out all the details, she hugged them goodbye and rushed back to her Ford Escape. She took a few moments to sit and breathe before starting toward the hospital. On the way, she used the hands-free feature to call her best friend, Nicole. "Girl, you are not going to believe my day!"

Chapter Nineteen

Entering the emergency department waiting room, Shelly couldn't believe it when she saw Nicole and Tim sitting near the sliding glass doors. "Nicole? What on earth? I didn't mean for you to take the whole day off work. Who has your class?" Without waiting for an answer, she pulled her into a huge hug.

Nicole laughed. "Several of our students' parents were getting their children out early. Due to this newest bombing, Mr. Lee, our principal, called for an early release. Since he knows you and I are such good friends, he let me go as soon as they dismissed the students. So, Tim and I are here to do whatever you need. In fact, Tim was just gonna run and get all of us some lunch."

"That sounds good, but I need to find Curly first. This place is completely insane today. Look at all these people waiting to be seen! I'm glad he decided to come in the ambulance, so he doesn't have to wait out here."

"Go ahead. Find him and see how he's doing. Tim and I will be waiting right here." Shelly went to the information desk and was handed a clipboard full of forms to fill out. The attendant informed her that only one person was allowed back with him, so after filling out the paperwork, she was given a guest badge and escorted back to the emergency department. She was shocked to see doctors and nurses running in every direction. They had so many patients that they had them on gurneys lining the hallways. She couldn't help rolling her eyes when she opened the door to Curly's room, and saw he was being examined by the same doctor she had after waking from her coma.

"Doctor Catania, fancy seeing you again so soon."

Shaking her hand, the doctor took a moment to check her eyes before responding, "Well, well. You two are quite a pair, aren't you? Mrs. Rogers, I really wish you were still resting at home. I would hate to see you have a relapse from all this worry and running around. However, I do understand why that's just not possible right now." He glanced toward Curly. " I just confirmed that your husband does indeed have a concussion as well. Although his is a very minor one compared to what you had. He just has a couple of places that require stitching. After that, he can go. But let me be very clear here. If he agrees to go home, he must rest for the next three days. No going into his office under any conditions. Agreed?"

Curly groaned and put his hands on his head. "Doc! Come on! Our mayor was just killed. And I don't even know who else! I don't have a choice; I MUST go into the office. Someone, meaning me, needs to lead this investigation."

The doctor crossed his arms and stood tall. "Sorry. It's either home for three days or I admit you. What's it going to be?"

"Fine! Home. Just don't go taking all day getting me discharged."

After the doctor left, Shelly gave him a kiss and fixed his hair. "Hey, grumpy, we can be concussion buddies!"

"Ha! Ha! I don't have time to be sick. Not that I wouldn't love some one-on-one time with my beautiful new wife, but I've got too much to do."

"None of us has time to be sick. Why don't I get Chad and those FBI guys to meet us at the house? That way, they can keep you updated?"

"Well, if I can't go into the office, I guess that's the next best thing. Thanks, hon. Some lieutenant I am. A second bombing in less than two weeks, and we have absolutely no idea whatsoever who is behind this Omega group. I feel horrible for the mayor's family. She's now a single mom with four kids, all because I didn't stop this from happening."

Before she could answer, another doctor entered and stitched up Curly's injuries. A few hours later when Shelly finally drove him home, they entered their apartment to find it full of people.

"Hey, bro! Man, am I glad you're okay!" Chad slapped him on the shoulder as he continued, "When Shelly texted what she wanted, I rounded everyone up. So, have a seat in that butt-ugly recliner. Willis and Tolley are in the kitchen trying to make us some coffee. Tim and Nicole are bringing a whiteboard over for us to track all the info that comes through."

Curly looked around as he leaned back in the recliner, amazed that so many officers and others were crammed into his living room. *We really need to find a bigger house.* "Wow! Thanks, everyone, for being willing to switch things up. Max! Down! Quit bothering…" Confused, Curly looked at Shelly, "I know I have a concussion, but I don't think I know that lady that Max is begging for cookies from."

Shelly shrugged, while Chad blushed and said, "Oh, yeah! Sorry. Hey, everyone, this is Joelle Oxford, my beautiful girlfriend. Joelle, this feeble old man is my brother, Lieutenant Rogers."

"Joelle, welcome. And just call me Curly. This is my wife, Shelly, and our son, Tucker, is back in his room. You'll have to catch up with all the rest of these yahoos some other time. Chad, why is this the first that I'm hearing of a girlfriend?"

"Um, well, ya see, um, you've been quite busy. We met while you were on that cruise getting married." The doorbell interrupted his bumbling explanation. "Ah! Saved by the bell!" Everyone chuckled as he opened it to find Pastor Thomas and a man he didn't know at the door.

"Chad, good to see you. I heard about what happened to your brother and thought I would check-in. Seems like all Pilotview had the same idea, so maybe…"

"No, no, it's fine. Come on in. He's over there in his chair."

Pastor Thomas greeted each person as he made his way over to Curly. "Curly, am I ever so thankful that God decided to spare your life today. This is Alan. Remember me telling you about him? I'll let you two talk. I mainly am here to see Tucker. Is he home?"

"Sure, I remember you mentioning him. Alan, you're a retired state trooper, correct? Nice to meet you. Pastor, Tuck is back in his room. Go on back."

* * *

As Curly and Alan talked, Pastor Thomas knocked on Tucker's bedroom door. "Mind if you and I hang out for a bit?"

Tucker shrugged while lying on his bed playing on his phone. "Sure, whatever. Am I in trouble or somethin'?"

Pastor Thomas pulled Tucker's desk chair over to the bed and sat down as he reassured him, "No, no, not at all. It's just when I heard about what happened to Curly today, the Lord laid you on my heart. Son, you've been through so much in your life. Adopted at birth, finding your mother murdered in your own kitchen, your father then being murdered, adopted again, then your new mom being in a coma and now your new dad was hurt at work. That's quite a load for even a strong, adult Christian to handle. I can't even begin to imagine how you are coping with all of this. Are you okay, son? Is there anything I can do? You know you can talk to me about anything, and it will stay between us."

When Tucker heard his pastor list all the things he had gone through in his life, he couldn't stop the tears from running down his face. "I...I'm not...I'm not okay. I mean, I keep praying and trying to trust Jesus like Mama Shelly has taught me, but why does this keep happening? It's me, isn't it? I'm the reason everyone around me keeps dyin' and gettin' hurt. It'd probably be best for everyone if I just wasn't even alive."

Chapter Twenty

The farmhouse smelled of warm mildew that crept into every corner of the building. Realizing he hadn't fed the women in over two days, he threw his game controller to the floor and stomped into the kitchen while kicking trash and debris out of his way. *This place is nastier than Gramps' pigsty up in Kentucky. Oh well, we should only be here another few days at the most. Should be getting a call sometime today to give me the schedule.* He grabbed the big soup pot that was still sitting on the stove from the last meal and without bothering to wash it, he filled it with water and put it back on the stove to boil. Once it was boiling, he threw in some of the meat he'd lifted from that old geezer the next road over. *'Bout outta meat. Gonna have to go lift some more if those women are gonna be here much longer.*

Just as he turned the heat down to simmer, he heard the crunch of tires on the gravel driveway. Hiking up his pants, he picked up his 20-gauge shotgun and pulled the corner of the torn curtain back so he could see who was in the driveway. Seeing it was his boss in his silver Yukon, and another man slouched in the passenger's seat, he relaxed a bit but waited to be sure. A couple of minutes later, his boss did indeed step out and stopped while putting his hands on his back to stretch.

While his boss was finishing stretching, he reached over and turned off the heat to the stew, then threw open the kitchen's side door. "Hey, Murray! Man, I didn't 'spect to see ya today. What's brought ya all the way up here from Fort Lauderdale?"

Murray reached into his truck, grabbed his duffel and gun and strode to the old, faded farmhouse. "First, grab me a beer while I go use your can." When he had returned and gotten as comfortable as was possible on the tattered, sagging, and ripped recliner, he took a long swallow before he began.

"That sure hits the spot. So, here's what's going on. The big boss saw on the news about those bombings up here and is very, very concerned about the cargo. So, we were sent up here from Florida just to keep an eye on things and to make sure the cargo is very well-taken care of before it's shipped off to Wilmington. There have been some changes in transportation," he said, taking another drink. "With your pick-up time still two weeks away, I've been ordered to do an inspection of the cargo. But first, are you the one doing these bombings?"

"Listen, man, all is good. No, not good. It's great! I was just finishing up boiling some meat to feed them. They're fine. Some of them are mighty fine. Know what I mean?" He swallowed his chuckle when he realized Murray wasn't amused but was glaring at him instead. Quickly, he continued, "Seriously, man, relax. It's all good; and, yes, I am behind the bombings."

Before he could continue, Murray exploded out of the recliner and slammed a fist into the man's chest, knocking him back several feet. "I KNEW it! During the whole long 13 hours that we were driving up here, I kept trying to tell myself you wouldn't be so stupid, but I KNEW you were! You are such a total screw-up! Give me one good reason I shouldn't shoot you dead right here for totally screwing up this mega-million dollar deal!"

"Um, well, I heard in town that the geezer I stole the meat from, Jed, went to the cops. I didn't want them sniffing around, so I decided the cops needed a distraction."

"A DISTRACTION? You ARE an IDIOT! Your stupidity has brought in the FBI, so now MORE cops are sniffing around. And who is this OMEGA group?"

"Um, well," shrugging and clearing his throat, the man gingerly stepped back as he answered, "Um, well, this way, they think that there's a group and won't be looking for one person. Just calm down."

He hesitated while taking a sip of water. "So, due to my day job, I have been able to overhear the Lieutenant's son talking to his buddies. The cops are stumped, so it worked exactly as I planned." The man paused, then nodded his head toward the doorway. "But I do need to go feed the women. Why don't we take them their lunch, and you can see for yourself that all is good?"

Murray glared at him for a full minute before turning away and waving his hand towards the kitchen. "Go ahead and be quick about it. I need to straighten this mess out so we can get back down to Fort Lauderdale for the next shipment up here. You are gonna have a full barn in just over a week. Get a list of supplies that you need while I go get Keno in here to help us feed the girls."

After finishing the stew, the men carried the pot out to the old tobacco barn set back in the woods at the very edge of the property.

Once there, Murray watched as the other man unlocked the padlock and slid the door open. Then, they brushed the hay to the side to reveal the concrete door in the floor. Once he had it opened, he stepped aside to let Murray precede him down the spiral steps to the underground dungeon. They had one much heavier concrete door to open once they reached the bottom of the steps. After opening it, Murray gasped at the stench that was released.

"I thought you said they were fine. That sure doesn't smell fine to me," he gagged.

"What do you expect when you have thirty or so women with nothing but buckets for toilets?" He stood aside as Murray slowly walked from cell to cell, inspecting each woman for any bruising or sickness. The women scurried like rats to the back of each cell and whimpered as they curled into balls.

Murray turned and waved him over. "You get to live another day as I don't see any injuries. However, they are getting way too skinny for the buyers. You are to begin feeding them twice a day. The boss expects you to handle securing the food and expects top-quality merchandise, so make sure you do this."

As they slopped lukewarm stew into the metal bowls attached to a lower bar in each cell, they discussed logistics for securing more meat. As they approached the last cell, a red light over the exit door lit up and started blinking.

"What's that light blinking for?" Murray asked.

"Get your gun. Tell Keno to get down here quick. We got trouble 'cause that means someone just turned into the drive. We need to go NOW."

Chapter Twenty-one

Back in Curly's den, the on-duty officers were busy strategizing their next move to track down the Omega group. Nick was busy transferring Curly's lists onto the whiteboard set up next to the fireplace while Curly and Agents Willis and Tolley worked on a map for Chad to start canvassing.

"Lieutenant, we don't usually condone the use of civilians for any type of police work, but since Chad is literally days away from his graduation, we agree that he's a good fit to handle the door-to-door near Jed's place. He can focus on tracking down whoever took the meat, and maybe something will pop up about the bombings. However, we do think it's vital that you deputize him first to avoid any legal fall-out down the road."

"Good idea. Chad, come over here for a sec would ya?" Once Chad had grabbed a stool from the bar area Curly continued, "Where's Joelle? I wanted to have a nice chat with her."

Chuckling, Chad stretched his long legs out as he responded, "Ha! I'm sure you do. She had to get back to City Hall; she was just here on her lunch break. She works in the water department. You can tell her all my deeply hidden and embarrassing secrets another time. So what's up?"

"She works at City Hall? How have I never seen her before?" Before Chad could begin to answer, Curly waved his hand to silence him and continued, "Later. Right now, we have a lot more important things to discuss. How far have you gotten on your canvassing out around Jed's place?"

"Not far at all. Seems like every time I head over there, an emergency happens, and I'm needed at the hospital to rescue your butt like always."

"Ha! Ha! In your dreams. Okay, the agents here have a great idea. We're gonna deputize you right now. Then, next week, when you have officially graduated from the academy, you'll be hired as a paid officer. Also, this has gotten way more serious than just some missing meat, so I need you to be extra diligent. No heroics. Anything at all that makes you the least bit suspicious, you call it in ASAP. Agreed?"

At Chad's nod of agreement, Curly had him raise his hand and take the oath. Having the legal necessities out of the way, Curly waved the agents over to show Chad where they wanted him to focus his canvas.

Chad took detailed notes, keeping his face as stoic as possible. He accepted the keys to the police SUV from Curly before striding briskly to the car, hoping no one noticed how excited he was to be a deputy.

Woo eee! An official deputy! Wait until Joelle hears about this! And a police officer next week! Finally! He paused for a moment, tightly gripping the keys. *Please, God, don't let me screw this up, and it would sure be great to find something, however little, to help Curly figure this out.*

A couple of hours later, he wasn't nearly as excited as he had been. After knocking on over a hundred doors in the sweltering, humid August heat, he just wanted the day to be done so he could go home, shower, and get a tall glass of cold, sweet tea. So far, all he had netted for his efforts were countless, empty homes or homes with senior citizens eager to ramble on about everything going on in their lives. There had been a handful of younger parents who answered, but they were too preoccupied with their small children that they weren't aware of things happening around them in their neighborhood.

He let out a huge groan as he pulled into the next paved driveway, spotting yet another white-haired lady kneeling in the front flower bed, pulling weeds. *Great! Another life story! Almost wish Curly would call with an emergency just to save me from this madness! Oh well, suck it up, Chad! Someone's got to do this and that someone is you!*

He stepped out of the car and walked over to the flower bed. Extending a hand, he introduced himself. "Good afternoon, ma'am. I'm Deputy Chad Rogers with the Pilotview Police Department. Do you have some time for a few questions?"

The lady pulled off her flowered gardening gloves, shook his offered hand, and nimbly rose to her feet, "Afternoon, Deputy. I am Hazel Angel. Why don't we go into the house and sit a spell so we can cool off with some fresh, ice-cold, homemade lemonade?"

After they were seated at her small kitchen table with their indeed very cold lemonades in hand in a kitchen so clean someone could perform surgery, Chad began going through the list of questions the agents and Curly had ordered him to ask. When he had finished his lemonade, he asked, "Have you seen anything suspicious in the last month?" Hazel put her glass down on the table, wiped some condensation off the side of the glass, and glanced out the front window.

After a few moments, she finally started to talk, "Deputy," she said slowly, "I must say as how I don't rightly like snooping on my friends and neighbors, but I have been plumb appalled at these bombings, so I will try to help you if I possibly can. I am home most days and spend most of my days outside with my flowers. This means that I know almost everybody on this street and their cars. I haven't really seen anything, or I would've called into the tip line. However, I, well, it's not really anything you police would be interested in, I'm sure."

"Ma'am, I'm sure it's nothing, but right now, we're interested in anything out of the ordinary. Go ahead and tell me what it is, and we'll decide if it's important or not," he encouraged by cocking his head to the side and smiling.

"Land sakes, Deputy, if I was just a few years younger, I would snatch you right up!" They laughed. "Again, it's really nothing to trouble you over when so much else is going on, but you know that abandoned property across the street? That farmhouse and barn that's been condemned by the city?" At his nod, she continued, "Well, all I was gonna say is that I've seen a couple of cars that I don't know going in and out of there. But I'm sure it's just the city officials checking it out before the demolition."

"It could be, but just in case it is important, could you describe these vehicles for me?" Chad's eyes widened as she provided a detailed description of a rusted, beat-up Ford Transit passenger van with missing windows in the back and on the sides. She then told him she had also noticed a silver Yukon going in and out as well.

"Yukon? Are you sure it's a Yukon?" Chad asked, leaning forward.

"Oh yes, my Bonnie, she's my daughter. Well, she drives one just like it. In fact, I actually thought it was her the first time I saw it turning in over there."

"When did you first see anyone going in that driveway?"

"Oh, Lord! I really can't say. Maybe three or four months ago?"

"This is great!" Chad quickly jotted down the information. "Is there anything else at all that you have found different or suspicious?"

"Well, I really feel foolish telling you this. After all, it's my own fault for not locking things up. But I keep an extra refrigerator out on my carport, and a few months back all my meat that I had stored up out there was just gone. Strangest thing I ever saw!"

More stolen meat? What on earth is going on around here? Chad finished the last few questions and his lemonade, then called Curly with an update as he went out to his car. "Curly, you are not going to believe what I have to tell you."

Chapter Twenty-two

Curly watched the last of his officers head out to their various assignments as Nick stayed behind to pack up all the items they'd brought from the police department. After he had loaded the last box and the cumbersome whiteboard into the back of his official pick-up truck, Curly stopped him as he started gathering the dirty coffee mugs.

"Man, just leave all that. I really appreciate you and all the others for setting this all up here. Made things a lot easier since I'm stuck here." He paused as he glanced around the tiny den, a room barely big enough for the faux leather loveseat and small recliner. "After having ya'll here today, I am going to have to get serious about finding us a bigger place. But never mind about all that. That's a problem for another time."

Curly stretched out his hand to shake Nick's. "Thanks again for everything. Just remember, the agents are going to use my office until I return in a couple days, so be sure to keep them, and me, in the loop. I'm here if you need anything at all."

"Ahem. No, Nick, he's not," Shelly interjected firmly. "I'm overriding that on doctor's orders. I shouldn't have let him participate in this meeting you all had today, but I know it was necessary. But that's it. I have his phone, and both of us are going to just stay here and recover. Right, honey?"

Shelly had been picking up the dirty coffee mugs but turned and raised an eyebrow at Curly, daring him to argue.

Nick laughed, raising his hands in surrender. "I think I best leave on that note. I promise, Mrs. Rogers, I won't be bothering ya'll at all. Take care." With that, he quickly backed out the door as Shelly carried the mugs into the kitchen to deal with later.

Once she had the mess in the den straightened up, Shelly joined Curly on the loveseat and snuggled up between him and Max. As she scratched Max behind the ears, she asked, "Now, what's this I heard about a bigger place? You know I love this place. Do you really think we need to move?"

Back in his bedroom, Tucker lay on his bed mentally running through all he and Pastor Thomas had discussed. He felt a bit better after talking to him, especially when the pastor prayed with him before he left. Despite the prayers, he just couldn't shake off that one thought that continued to haunt him: why it seemed like anyone he loved always died.

God, I just don't understand all this. I thought I had gotten over losing my mama and daddy, but then Shelly got knocked out and almost died, and now Curly almost died. Why? Is it me? What have I done to deserve everyone I love dyin' and gettin' hurt? How come everyone else I know gets to have a normal family with both parents, grandparents, aunts, uncles, and cousins, and I have no one? It's just not fair. I know Pastor said it's not my fault, but he's just saying that to make me feel better. I bet if Curly and Mama Shelly had never met me that none of this awful stuff woulda happened to them. They'd be better off if I had been at City Hall today and died in that bombing.

Tucker rolled over, burying his freckled face into his pillow to muffle his gut-wrenching sobs. A few minutes later, he felt Max's cold, wet nose nudging his head. Lifting his head, he wiped his eyes with his arm as Max whined softly at Tucker's sniffling.

Scooting over, Tucker tapped the bed so Max could jump up and lie next to him. "Hey! Stop whining! Thanks, buddy. I can always count on you to try to cheer me up." After giving Tucker's face a very thorough washing, Max jumped down and raced out of the room.

Moments later, Max returned and sat down expectantly with his green tennis ball in his mouth as he swished his tail on the carpet. He sat there staring at Tucker in anticipation. When Tucker didn't take the hint, he nudged it closer to the bed, whining persistently.

"Okay, okay! I get the hint! I guess I'll postpone my pity party and throw your ball for you. Let's take it outside so we don't get in trouble." At the word "outside," Max got so excited he took off running, barking all the way to the front door where he continued to bark and prance impatiently in circles. When Tucker finally found his tennis shoes and joined Max at the front door, Shelly spoke up from the couch.

"You two going outside? I'm making…wait," her tone shifted. "Tuck? What's wrong? Have you been crying?"

"It's nothin'! Let's go, Max! Come on!" Tucker opened the door and threw the ball high into the air and couldn't help cheering when the dog caught it in mid-air. He slammed the door shut behind him, hoping Shelly would forget all about her questions by dinner.

"Curly? Did you see his face? Something's wrong. He looks like he's been crying all day! Do you know what's going on? I best go talk to him."

As she started to stand, Curly reached out and gently tugged her back down. "Shell, give him some space. It's been a rough couple of weeks for all of us. Plus, I saw Pastor Thomas in there earlier talking with him. I'll speak with him after dinner tonight. Meanwhile, I'm enjoying our snuggle time together."

Chapter Twenty-three

Back in his SUV, Chad sat for a few minutes to let the air conditioning cool the interior while he jotted down a few more notes about his interview with Hazel. He wanted to prove himself to his older brother so badly that he debated whether to check out the property she had mentioned.

It's probably nothing and will be just another huge waste of time, but Curly did say he wanted to hear about any little thing that was suspicious no matter how small.

Frustrated, Chad groaned. "Ugh. This is stupid!" he muttered, yanking his cell phone from the dash mount. He was surprised when Curly actually answered, assuming Shelly had turned his phone off. *Must've snuck it away from her. Good!*

"Curly, Chad here. You said to inform you about anything suspicious. Well, there's this old lady over here on Hillview Drive who has also had her carport freezer broken into and the meat stolen just like Jed. She also says there's been a couple of cars that she doesn't recognize going in and out of a property across the way from her. I'm heading over that way now that I have checked in with you."

"Another elderly person missing meat? I just don't understand why someone would steal from the elderly! When you get a chance, write up your notes and send them to me. I'll get a tech over there to process the freezer. And hold off on checking out that property. In fact, head on over to headquarters and I'll have Officer Nick meet you. I would feel better if you had backup on this."

"Curly, come on! You can't be serious? Doesn't he have anything better to do? After all, this is all probably just Mrs. Angel's overactive imagination. You know how these retired, old ladies love attention and dreaming up stories about their neighbors! There's no sense wasting Nick's time going with me when I am right here."

"Did you say Mrs. Angel? I happen to know her quite well, and she is one very sharp lady! She's helped me out a few times, and if she's saying these cars haven't been there before, then they haven't. And a word of advice, bro: sometimes the older generation pays closer attention to their surroundings. Don't automatically write something off just because the person telling you is older than you. They usually know their neighborhood very well. So do as I say and head into headquarters."

Sighing, Chad rubbed a hand over his short, brown crew cut, his frustration evident as he slammed the phone back in its holder, then proceeded back to downtown Pilotview.

I'm right here. But no! I have to wait on a babysitter to help me talk to people. If he would just listen to me! I can't wait until I'm an official officer next week and don't have to be treated with kid gloves anymore.

As Chad walked into the police station, Sheila called out from the front desk. "Hey, hon! Nick wanted me to tell you he's out running an errand and should be here shortly. Why don't you take a break and have one of my famous banana muffins? You look like you could use one."

"Well, sure! Thanks! I missed lunch, so if it's okay with you, I'll take two."

"Hon, you take as many as you need. Can't have you passin' out on us from a blood sugar drop." She patted his arm as she answered the ringing phone.

Grabbing his muffins and a napkin, Chad strode down the hall to the conference room, shooting a quick text to Joelle to confirm dinner plans. Realizing it was eerily quiet, he looked around and found he was the only person in the back section of the station. The Pilotview police department was usually bustling with citizens and officers coming and going all the time. Phones were usually ringing non-stop, and there was usually a drunk or two yelling, but today, the place felt empty due to Curly having all hands on deck and everyone out on assignments.

Taking advantage of the downtime, he typed up his notes from the morning interview, emailing them to Curly so that he would have a record, which he felt was a huge waste of time. Just as he finished and opened his solitaire app to play a few rounds, Nick's voice echoed down the hall. "Chad? You back there? Come on! No time to waste!"

"I'm here!" Chad quickly strode back down the hall to the front and saw Nick leaning on the counter, chatting with Sheila as he scarfed down one of her muffins.

"Hey, Nick! Don't eat them all 'cause I want another one. Those things are amazing! Thanks again, Sheila! You're a lifesaver!"

"Oh, go on now, you two! Quit flattering this old lady."

"Old lady? Where?" Chad replied with a wink and smile before following Nick out to his cruiser.

"Sorry about you being saddled with a cadet. Am sure you would rather be out doing real police work instead of babysitting me." Chad buckled up as Nick entered the destination into the laptop secured to the dash.

"Eh, no worries. I'm just a rookie myself, so that's why the Lieutenant gives me all the scutt jobs. By the way, he told me that this Mrs. Angel, Hazel, is pretty sharp, so you never know. This just might turn into something. Hey, any chance you know a Bob Roland who's at the academy? I think he is graduating next week, too."

"Yeah, I know him. He's a good guy. And he's amazing with anything related to technology. How do you know him?"

Nick laughed. "We were in the Marines together. Let me tell you about him!"

The rest of the drive was spent swapping stories and talking about the academy. When they arrived on Hillview Drive, Chad spotted Hazel weeding her flower bed. She looked up and gave them a cheerful wave as they drove past.

"That's Hazel Angel. She's the one who's also had meat stolen from her freezer. She's a pretty sharp lady. She is the one who spotted those vehicles," Chad said. Then he pointed ahead. "Stop! There's the entrance to the property right there between those overgrown hydrangea bushes."

Chapter Twenty-four

"Hey, girl! What's going on?" Shelly asked, answering her phone.

"You aren't gonna believe the news I just got!" Nicole squealed so loudly that Curly could hear her from across the room. "Remember me telling ya about my Uncle Don passing away a couple of months ago?"

"Of course I remember. But surely that isn't causing you to squeal this loud!"

"Well, the attorney handling his estate just called and informed me that Uncle Don left me his beautiful home over on Sauratown Bluff! Eeek! I'm still having trouble wrapping my mind around this! Once I sign all the paperwork tomorrow, I'll be a homeowner. Tim and I are gonna finally have our own place! Can you believe it?"

Shelly laughed at Nicole's squeals. "Congratulations! That's awesome. Wait! How's that gonna work with your dad and his place? I know he's not capable of staying there by himself. You gonna move him to your new place with you? Is it big enough?"

Nicole sighed loudly as she answered, "I forgot that I haven't caught you up with all that's been going on. That's the 'not-so-exciting news.' Dad's Alzheimer's has gotten drastically worse, and he's starting to fall quite a bit. Last week, Tim and I decided it's time for us to find an assisted living facility for him. You know how much I hate the thought of putting him in one of those facilities, Shell, but it's just gotten to be too much for us, with both of us working. And my sister and brother can't be bothered to take him in. We really think it's best, especially for his safety."

"Oh, Nicole! I'm so sorry! I can't even begin to imagine how difficult that decision must have been for ya'll, but I have to say I agree—it's the best thing to do. But if you move to Sauratown Bluff, what will you do with his place? Sell it?"

"Ugh! I really don't want to sell his place. I talked it over with the family and they don't care what I do with it. The place doesn't really hold any special memories for any of us because he bought it after Mom passed away and he retired. It's just that Tim and I love the views up at Sauratown Bluff up at our uncle's place so much better, and its just been updated and renovated a couple of years back. I really don't have any idea what we're gonna do. You have any ideas?"

"Actually? I do have one!" Shelly smiled. "Curly has been going on about how we need a bigger place. What would you say to us renting it from you? Maybe even rent to own?"

"Why on earth didn't I think of that? That would be perfect all around. I really dreaded dealing with renters, but ya'll would be the perfect answer!"

"Hold on before you go getting too excited! I need to run all of this by him first. Why don't I get him and Tuck and we'll meet you out there in, say, an hour?" she asked as she looked up at the clock above the fireplace.

"Of course! Eeek! I'm getting excited anyway. I just know it's gonna work out! See ya in an hour!"

Laughing at her friend's squeals, Shelly concluded the call and turned to Curly, who had obviously heard the whole conversation since Nicole had been shouting over the phone. "I'm sure you heard all that. What do you think? You want to live on a small farm?"

Curly took a moment before answering to reach out and wrap a strand of her hair around his finger. "Anything that has more space than this tiny apartment would be great, but we'll need to discuss this with Tucker first, don't we?'

"Discuss what with me?" Tucker asked, stepping into the room as he popped open a can of Dr. Pepper with Max trotting on his heels.

"Tuck! I thought you and Max were still outside," Shelly said as she sat up and scooted over on the couch to see him better.

"Yeah, I jest came in to get some soda and heard ya say ya needed to discuss something with me. What's going on? Something else bad happen?" he asked, plopping down onto the recliner with his legs hanging over the side.

"Well, no, nothing bad," Shelly said quickly. "Actually, we may have good news. It looks like Nicole's dad is going to assisted living, which isn't great news, but we've all been expecting that to happen soon. The exciting part is what we want to discuss with you! Nicole just found out that her Uncle Don left her his house. She and Tim are gonna move into it once she gets her dad situated. She asked us to consider renting her dad's place. What would you think about that? Would you be okay with moving out of here and out to the country?"

"Heck, yeah! Her dad's place is awesome! That skinny spiral staircase in the back of the dining room that goes upstairs has always been one of my favorite places to play. Hey, can I get the room upstairs? You know, the one with the ceiling that slants down?"

Curly held up his hand, "Slow down, son. Let's go look at the place then decide if it will all work before we start claiming rooms. Go get Max some fresh water and fill his food bowl. Then go get cleaned up so we can leave in about thirty minutes." After Tucker left to do as he was told, Curly stood and offered his hand to Shelly to help her up from the couch. "Well, sounds like he's all on board with moving."

"Sure sounds that way." Before she could continue, she heard his phone ringing and groaned. "Oh no! I'll give you your phone, but remember you're on doctor's orders to rest, and I need you to go out to Nicole's dad's place to give me your inpu. . .."

"I know, hon. It's Chad, so it should just take a minute." He swiped the green button and answered the call, "Chad! How did everything go for you and Nick out on Hillview?"

"Well, Curly, a big fat zero. No one answered our knocks, but someone's definitely living here. This place is supposed to be abandoned, but there are all kinds of tire tracks left in the dirt driveway. Then when we didn't get any answer, Nick and I walked around the place, and looking through the windows, we saw a television with an Xbox hooked up to it and a beat-up couch. There're also all kinds of soda cans lying all over the floor along with empty fast-food bags. What do you want us to do?"

Chapter Twenty-five

Murray impatiently smacked the man on the back of the head as he shouted, "What are you just standing there for? Go! Go!"

The man raised his hand and clenched his fist, "Wait," he commanded quietly, motioning to a small monitor at the top of the spiral stairs. "That's a cop. I had heard they were doing a door-to-door but never expected them to come by this place."

They froze, eyes locked on the monitor as the officer knocked on the house's front door, waited a few seconds, then knocked again. After he walked around the perimeter of the house, they watched him give up and head back to his vehicle. The men let out huge sighs of relief as they began to relax.

"What's he doing now? Why isn't he leaving? Wait! There's someone else in the car, and he's getting out!"

Murray nudged the man aside and leaned closer to get a better look at the monitor. Grabbing his cohort's shoulder, he growled, "If they get curious about the barn and head this way, we are taking them down. Understood? No matter what, they are *not* setting foot inside this barn."

The man nodded. "Agreed. I believe that's Lieutenant Rogers' brother with that cop." The three men raised their weapons to be ready to fire as they continued watching the other men's perusal of the house. After several tense minutes, they all visibly relaxed again when they watched the officers get in their car and leave.

Murray lowered his weapon and turned to the other man. "Listen, Marshall, there's no telling how long until they return. They had to notice your things in the house and are probably wondering why no one answered when my car and your pickup are parked right there. I'll have one of my sources bring the box van over."

Keno glanced at his watch. "Tell him to be here in thirty minutes. We're loading this shipment and heading to Wilmington in an hour. From there, you and I are catching a flight down to Fort Lauderdale for further orders from Ms. Baptiste."

Without waiting for a response, Murray turned and climbed up the stairwell into the dilapidated barn as he put his call in to one of his guys.

The dungeon resembled an underground horse stable with four separate prison-like cells lining each side and a wide path down the middle. There were four women crammed into each six-by-eight cage. Each woman was linked to another with a heavy chain like one would use to secure an aggressive dog in a yard. They were also shackled with an iron cuff attached to a chain. The woman on the end of the chain was then shackled to the wall.

With no air conditioning or proper ventilation, the stench was overwhelming. The women had no toilets or running water—just a handle-less five-gallon bucket in each cage for waste and another bucket he would occasionally remember to refill with drinking water.

When the women had first arrived, they had banged on the bars and walls while yelling and demanding to be released. As time went by, they gradually gave up yelling and banging as they grew weaker and weaker, on top of losing all hope that they would ever be rescued. They were living in conditions worse than most pets; they looked worse than neglected animals.

After getting a box van on the way, Murray stepped into the middle of the aisle between the cells and barked, "Listen up. I'm going to have this woman here in the first cage come and unlock each of you. Once you're free, you are to line up here in the aisle where I will give another one of you a hose to wash the filth off you. There is a stack of hospital gowns at the bottom of the steps that you are to change into after your shower. Just because you're unlocked, don't get any ideas. I'll have my gun on you the entire time and will shoot first and ask questions later."

Dragging the water hose down the steps, the man unlocked the first cage and went straight to the smallest girl. Unlocking her shackle, he roughly grabbed her by the arm and jerked her to her feet, shoving the key in her face. "You. Go unlock everyone, and no funny business," he sneered, waving his weapon. "Remember, I have my gun pointed at you." Then, he strode out and took his position at the end of the aisle, lifting the shotgun to his shoulder as he watched his orders being followed.

Exactly thirty minutes later, he heard the squeaky brakes of the white panel truck as it pulled into the barn and backed into the dungeon's opening. Murray stood guard, watching as the women shuffled up the staircase, where Keno stood with his weapon pointed at the barn's opening. Keno watched as the women timidly climbed out, blinking in the bright light, before crawling into the back of the truck, futilely clutching the backs of their gowns to keep them closed.

The last woman was pulled into the truck and collapsed. Keno then slammed the doors shut and secured them with a heavy padlock. He waited for his comrade to complete his final sweep of the dungeon before he climbed into the driver's seat. Pulling out of the barn, Keno and Murray nodded at Marshall as they started the long drive to Wilmington.

Marshall quickly gathered his things, locked up the barn and house and sped away from Hillview Drive as fast as possible.

If only they had not rushed the loading and had taken just a little more time to clean and sanitize more thoroughly, they might have noticed an odd pile tucked back in a dark corner of the dungeon's furthest cell from the stairs. After the echoes of their departure faded, the pile slowly started to move.

Chapter Twenty-six

Don't move! Don't move! Don't move! Oh God! It sounds like he's in the next cage. Please, God, don't let him look behind these buckets. Don't let him lift these rags off me.

I could sure use a huge distraction right about now, God. And I could really use a miracle the size of the one where you kept those lions from eating Daniel down in that pit that Grandma June was always telling me about. Oh, God, I'm so scared!

How did I end up in this mess after I was so careful? I just know Mom and Dad must be freaking out, wondering where I am. Please, please, please make me invisible!

Oh no! It sounds like he's even closer now, like he's right next to me. God! Help me!

Holding her breath, she continued her silent begging, desperately pleading to God, her heart pounding as footsteps came closer and closer. *He's going to find me.* Right when she was certain he would find her, she stifled a squeal when another voice echoed from upstairs.

"What is taking you so long, man? Those cops could come back at any moment. Take the lead out and get a move on!"

"All right! I'm coming! I'm coming!" the man snapped. "Was just finishing up down here." With a final glance at the filthy rags, discarded clothing, and overflowing, foul-smelling buckets of waste, the man sprinted up the metal stairs and slammed the door shut.

What? No way! He didn't see me. How is that even possible? Is he gone?

Then her breath caught. *What if I'm wrong? Stay still, Kimmy; it could be another one of his tricks! What if he's just standing there waiting for you to stand up so he can shoot you? But it feels and sounds like I'm all alone down here. The only thing I hear is that truck running. No matter. I best play it safe and lie here a while longer and be very still until I'm sure that I'm alone. I just hope he forgot to lock that door!*

Squeezing her eyes shut, she willed her trembling body to be still, refusing to move until the silence felt safe.

As the truck noises faded into the distance, she forced herself to count to one thousand before allowing herself to move. The cold cement floor made her rail-thin body ache, yet she continued to count.

One-thousand.

Having reached her goal, Kimmy cautiously opened one eye and then the other and waited a little more while straining to catch any sounds of another person. When all she could hear was the pounding of her own heart beating loudly, she ever so slowly lifted her head while pushing aside the rags. Her eyes were darting in every direction, knowing that at any moment, someone could pounce on her and kill her.

Still not convinced it was possible that she was truly alone, she gingerly stood, gripping the bars for support as her cramped legs trembled under her weight. *I DID IT! I DID IT! I escaped! Well, almost…just need to figure out how to get out of this filthy hole.*

Her thoughts raced. *I can't believe he didn't see me! That had to be you, God. There's no other explanation than a miracle. You caused his cohort to yell out to him the moment that I needed him distracted. A huge thank you for that!*

Determined, she glanced around the dungeon. *Now I need to find some clothes to put on so I can go find a cop. They have to stop that truck before those women are sold and gone forever!*

* * *

Two months earlier, Kimmy was having a great day at her job as a tram operator for Flamingo Gardens in Davie, Florida. She adored her job of interacting with all kinds of exotic animals. But she especially loved seeing the children's eyes light up when they spotted the many vibrant peacocks strutting about, fanning their dazzling plumage while honking to each other, or sometimes they would race the tram while honking at each other.

Her favorite part of the day, though, was her lunch break at the grill. That's when Jake, a precocious flamingo, would always strut over, stomping his feet and squawking loudly if she dared to ignore him. He knew she always carried a small bag with a couple of sardines just for him. After devouring his treat, he'd affectionately peck her head and grunt softly as if saying "thank you," before sauntering back to join the other flamingos in the pond. Then he would keep his eye out for unsuspecting visitors that he could sneak up on and steal their food.

That day at the grill, after the flamingo had stomped away, one of the guests sat at the picnic table adjacent to hers and struck up a conversation about Jake. The man asked all kinds of questions, but Kimmy didn't think much about it—she was used to park visitors being curious and asking a myriad of questions throughout the day.

Later that afternoon, she noticed the same guest sitting in the seat directly behind her on the final safari tram tour. When he stayed behind at the end to continue talking to her, she couldn't help but feel flattered that he seemed interested in her. *Maybe he's gonna ask me out! I sure hope so! He's so cute!*

He looked to be close to her age and was quite attractive with jet-black hair and dark brown, almost black eyes. She noticed he wore designer khaki shorts, a crisp golf shirt, and expensive Ray-Ban sunglasses.

After her shift ended, Kimmy was very pleasantly surprised to see the same man sitting at a table outside of the gift shop exit.

"You said your name was Keno, right? If I didn't know better, Keno, I would think that you're stalking me!" she joked, laughing as she sat across from him while taking a long drink from her bottle of water.

Smiling, he stretched out his legs casually. "Oh no. No stalking. Just waiting for you to finish work so I could ask you out for dinner. Are you free this evening? I'm sure you must be starving."

"Yeah, I'm famished," she admitted. "But I need to change first because it's been a very hot day, and these clothes have had it."

"No problem. I can follow you to your place and wait in the

car for you to change." He stopped talking as she started shaking her head.

"No, no. I'll meet you at the restaurant. And I don't want anything fancy. Just grab some dinner, and then I need to head home 'cause I have to be back here again really early tomorrow."

After agreeing to meet her, they decided to meet at the El Camino in just over an hour.

Smiling and humming, Kimmy shot off a quick text to her mom back home in Florida before she left the gardens.

> Just met a totally cute guy, Keno. Have a date with him tonight. And, yes, I'm being safe. Am meeting him there. Here's a picture I snapped when he wasn't looking. Isn't he hot?

Chapter Twenty-seven

Oh no! I'm late for work! Why didn't I hear my alarm? Wait! This isn't my bed, is it? Where on earth am I? Think, Kimmy! Struggling to fight off a rising panic attack, she tried to sit up and open her eyes but had to stop when huge waves of nausea overcame her. But in the brief time that her eyes were open, she didn't recognize anything in the room. *This isn't my room or my bed. Did I spend the night at Cami's house or maybe Mom's? No, that can't be right either. Nothing looks familiar. Think, Kimmy!*

As she lay there trying to remember where she was and how she had gotten there, she focused on the sounds around her. At first, all she could hear was her labored breathing, but after taking several long, slow breaths, other sounds began to emerge—the faint echo of children laughing and squealing and what sounded like waves crashing on the beach, but all of it sounded very far away. Then, much closer, she heard a faint whimper that wasn't far from her at all!

"Hello?" she called out, trembling. "Is anyone else here? Please, you must help me; I'm very sick." Determined to see who was in the room with her, Kimmy tried squinting without moving her head, hoping to keep the nausea away. *Nothing! All I can see is a nasty blanket and a dirty wall! I KNOW I heard someone!* After several more minutes of faint beach noises, she heard another soft whimper.

"Please, please! My name is Kimmy! I live in Fort Lauderdale, and as I said earlier, I'm very sick. I know someone is here with me. Please talk to me!" At first, all she heard were the beach sounds, but then, from her left, a very faint whisper.

"Sssshhhh! If he hears us, we'll get a beating for sure and no food! You can't make him mad. Please don't talk."

"But, I don't understand. What are you talking about? And who are you?"

"Please lower your voice!" the woman hissed. "He could come back at any time. I heard him say he was going to get more girls. The other guy calls him Murray, but the other guy doesn't usually talk to us. From what they were saying, they're gonna sell us to some rich guys in North Carolina."

"Sell me? Um, no way! No, nope! That ain't gonna happen!" Kimmy exclaimed. "I don't care if I am sick; I'm out of here!" She attempted to jump off the bed but quickly realized that her leg was chained to the wall. The sudden movement triggered another huge wave of nausea, and she doubled over as her stomach emptied itself.

"My name's Chelsea, and I'm sorry you're so sick. It's what they drugged you with. They did the same thing to me a few weeks ago. Now that you've been sick, you should start to feel better." Chelsea gasped. "Sssshhhh!! He's coming! I hear him on the steps!"

As Kimmy took several deep, shaky breaths to try and settle her stomach, the door flew open with a deafening crash as it slammed into the wall. The cute guy she was supposed to meet for dinner, Keno, was standing there next to the biggest, scariest-looking white guy she had ever seen. He was covered in tattoos and had a bandana wrapped around his head, but it was his eyes that truly terrified her—empty, cold, and devoid of anything human. Pure evil.

Kimmy bit her lip to keep from screaming as the man grabbed her chain, yanking it hard to ensure it was secure. Satisfied, he then turned toward the other bed. He knelt, jabbing his finger into Chelsea's chest "What ya been telling her? Huh? Tell me!"

Whimpering, Chelsea shrank back as far as her chain would allow, curling into a little ball while shaking her head frantically.

"Girl! I done asked ya a question! Answer me!" He lightly smacked her across the face then yelled, "I said, answer me!"

During this exchange, Keno had been leaning against the back of the door, but as he saw his buddy start to manhandle Chelsea, he cleared his throat and straightened. "Murray, stop."

"Stop what? Someone's gotta teach this brat here a lesson!" Murray answered without bothering to turn and look at Keno.

"Murray," Keno said evenly, "may I remind you that she's merchandise, and our buyers *do not* want damaged goods. Just give them their food, and let's go. We're on a tight schedule here, and there's a lot more to do before we leave town. We still have a lot more rooms to check. So cool it."

Kimmy had kept her eyes closed, trying to remain as quiet and small as possible. Suddenly, someone yanked her hair, making her gasp. She then sensed someone very close to her, so she opened her eyes to see Keno staring at her.

"Yeah, I knew you were playing possum. Sorry about our date."

Keno chuckled darkly before continuing, "Right now, you aren't gagged because we knew you'd be sick. We don't want to gag you, and we won't IF you behave. But if you scream, even once, or make a scene, you WILL be gagged. Do you understand me?" At her frightened nod, he went on, "Good. We'll be leaving in a little over an hour, so don't get too comfy. We brought you some broth to calm your stomach down. So eat!"

She stared at him, shaking. "Is your name really Keno? And why are you doing this to me? What did I ever do to you?"

"Keno is all that you need to know. As for the rest?" He shrugged as he answered, "You have a smile men will pay millions for. Nothing personal. Now I don't see you eating. Eat."

"No! I won't. I'm sick, and I don't want it," she snapped.

Keno smirked, then turned toward his partner. "Murray, you hear that? She told me no! That is quite funny. Why don't you tell her what happens when someone tells me no?"

Murray chuckled, "They live to regret it. Things get very painful."

Keno leaned closer, his eyes boring into hers. "That's right. Kimmy, listen carefully. There are a million other pretty girls out there that I could replace you with. If you ever tell me no again, that will be the last word that you ever speak on this earth. Now, for the last time—eat. We don't have time for this."

The look on his face sent chills down her spine. Without another word, Kimmy quickly picked up the cheap plastic spoon and started slurping the broth as fast as she could.

Oh God! Why did I ever think that he was cute? I should have listened to Mom! I should never have gone to meet him by myself. I'm sorry, Mom. I hope you can forgive me one day. And, please, God, please help me figure out a way to get out of this room!

Chapter Twenty-eight

A couple hours later, Murray and another man that Kimmy didn't recognize returned and unshackled the girls from the wall. They were marched outside to a white box van parked as close to the motel as possible. The van looked ordinary, like any other white work van on the road, with no windows in the back and ladders strapped to the roof.

As they forced the girls into the back, Kimmy's heart sank upon realizing they were on Hollywood Beach, just down the road from her home in Fort Lauderdale. The motel where they'd been held captive looked like any other unassuming place by the beach.

Look at all those families having a normal, fun day at the beach! They don't even realize what's happening right here in front of them, Kimmy thought. *Please, look this way.*

Just then, Murray tightened his grip on her arm and leaned down to whisper in her ear, "And don't even think about making a scene. Remember what Keno told you."

Kimmy gulped, rubbing the spot where his hand had left a mark. Climbing into the back of the van, she froze. Dozens of terrified women stared back from the dim interior, their faces pale with fear. At least thirty or even more women were crammed on the floor with their ankles and wrists bound with zip ties. Before

Kimmy could take it all in, Murray shoved her to the floor and swiftly secured her and Chelsea's wrists and ankles.

Once they were secure, Murray turned toward the other man. "Where's Keno? They should be here by now! This is going to put us behind."

"He just texted and said his ETA is five minutes. He had to stop and fill up the van 'cause he forgot to do it last night. Look! There's his van turning in now. Let's get this show on the road!"

The men jumped into the vehicle, and as Murray cranked the engine, he raised his voice to make sure all the women could hear him. "We have a twelve-to-thirteen-hour ride ahead of us. We'll stop every three hours for you to relieve yourselves. Don't get any ideas of running. We have guns and will shoot you without warning. Also, don't get any ideas about getting someone's attention at the stops. Because all our stops will be at homes that we own set out in the country far from anyone. I suggest you all try to sleep because you will be quite busy once we arrive."

Kimmy's chest tightened as the words sank in. *This can't be happening to me!* Her thoughts were spiraling into panic. *I knew this area of Florida is a huge sex and human trafficking area, but I've been SO careful! The ONE time I dropped my guard just a little bit, I'm going to be sold. It's just not fair!*

Tears welled in her eyes as she whispered a desperate prayer. *God, please, please I just want to go home and watch* Jag *with Mom and Dad and have Sammie curled up next to me purring. Please, show me a way out of this nightmare!*

* * *

Present time

Nick and Chad sat behind Mrs. Angel's shed, watching the property across the street. When Curly had assigned them to conduct surveillance, Nick had groaned and complained loudly, while Chad fought to hide his grin, secretly thrilled to be on another "cool" police assignment.

Nick had tried to convince Curly that his talents would be put to better use by tracking down leads on the bombings, but when Curly refused to budge, Nick just threw up his hands in frustration and motioned for Chad to follow him out to Chad's personal car.

Before heading to their post, the pair stopped at the local 7-11 to stock up on various snack foods and drinks. When Nick told Chad to grab a couple of sports magazines as well, Chad asked, "What? We preparing for a blizzard in August or something? What on earth do we need with all this stuff?"

"Ha! You have much to learn, my little grasshopper! Surveillance is right up there with paperwork as the absolute most boring and butt-numbing part of police work. You will see that this is just going to be a bunch of sitting around being bored for hours on end. And even though your eyes and body are tired, you are expected to stay at full alert just in case something should happen, which it rarely does." Smacking Chad on the shoulder, he continued, "So go grab us a couple of large black coffees 'cause we need all the caffeine we can get. Meet you at the car."

At first, the shift wasn't so bad. While Chad kept watch, Nick would take breaks, make calls, fill out paperwork, use Mrs. Angel's restroom, or stretch his legs. Then they would switch off.

Chad had already stopped texting Joelle because she was in a meeting at work. After catching up on his emails, he was left with magazines and chit-chat. So, after telling each other every stupid thing that they had ever done, they were now discussing every detail they knew about the bombings to try to figure out if the missing meat had anything to do with that.

"Nick, I know I've not graduated yet," Chad said, absentmindedly flipping through a magazine, "but this just feels like a huge waste of time. All we saw over there was some trash and food leftovers. Seems to me it's just some kids using it as a hangout spot."

"You could be right, and you probably are. But I've learned to never second-guess the boss. I know he's your big brother, but over the years, I've seen how he's usually right about these things. It's like he has a second sense about it." Nick sighed, rubbing his temples. "However, I'm hoping you're right and it's just kids trespassing and making a mess, but my gut says something else is going on over there. Just too big of a coincidence for this to be going on at the same time as the bombings."

"Okay, I hear ya. I'm getting tired of junk food. I need a meal. Why don't I run back to the 7-11 and get some ham sandwiches?"

"Sure. I like mine with mayo, mustard, and cheese. Why don't you grab us some cold Cokes while you're at it? Don't take too long, though, and keep your radio on."

Chad gave him a thumbs up and jogged to his car parked in Mrs. Angel's garage. Nick couldn't help shaking his head and chuckling at Chad's rookie enthusiasm as he watched him leave. *Rookies! He's gonna need to learn to sit still and be bored if he's gonna make detective one day.*

Chapter Twenty-nine

Curly, Shelly, Tucker, and Max had just finished their tour of Nicole's dad's farm. Well, Max was still out chasing rabbits and birds, but the rest followed Nicole and Tim into the large country kitchen and settled around the long farmhouse-style table. Nicole and Shelly brought out sweet tea and homemade chocolate chip cookies for everyone.

"Well, what's the verdict?" Nicole asked. "Do you want to live here? I know what you currently pay for rent since the church is your landlord, and we're planning on charging the same amount with no security deposit." She took a sip of her tea and reached for Tim's hand as she continued. "Shell, it would mean so much to us to know ya'll are living here. If you can't tell, we really want ya'll to say yes!"

Shelly and Curly laughed as Shelly added, "No pressure, though, right? Well, Nikki, I know how I feel and what I would say, but I think I need to talk this over with my fellas first."

"Shell, hon, I am one hundred percent on board with the idea," Curly said. "Look how much more room we would have! Max obviously loves it here! He and Tucker would have so much more space to run and explore. But we will be quite a bit further from town and Tuck's friends." Curly turned toward the boy. "What do you think, son? Be honest. We truly want to know your feelings about moving here. If you'd rather we find us a place in town, then that's what we'll do. You've had enough big changes in your life, so we want this to be what you feel comfortable doing."

"Heck, yeah! I done told ya that I love it here, and I've done picked out my room upstairs. Please say yes!"

Curly reached over and ruffled Tucker's carrot top as he winked at Shelly. "Well, hon, I think that's unanimous. It's a yes!"

Nicole let out an excited squeal, whooping so loudly that Max came scampering in to see what all the commotion was about. Seeing everyone was sitting at the table eating, he immediately went to Tucker's side. Putting his right paw on Tucker's knee, the dog gave a perfectly executed pitiful look, hoping for a morsel of cookie.

Tucker laughed, ruffling Max's fur, and said, "Can I be excused? I want to go show Max his room."

Shelly brushed tears from her eyes as Tucker and Max raced up the stairs. "Nikki, that's the happiest I've seen him in a long, long time. How about you get your lawyer to set everything up and we'll sign the papers? I can already see myself cooking meals in this amazing kitchen. You all did a wonderful job updating it. You, dear friend, are an answer to a prayer that I haven't even prayed yet."

"Well, hon, you might not have prayed for it yet, but I have!" Curly said. "Seeing all those officers crammed into our living room earlier made me realize it even more. Thank ya'll so much for this amazing offer!" He leaned back in his chair as he reached for Shelly's hand. "I agree with my beautiful wife. I'm ready as soon as ya'll get all the legalities taken care of."

"So, about that…" Nicole took a long pause while she took a bite of cookie and a large drink of tea.

Shelly said, "Nikki, stop being so dramatic! Out with it already!"

Chuckling at their expressions and groans, Nicole held her hand up as she answered, "Okay, okay. I was so sure that ya'll would want to live here that I already had our lawyer draw up all the papers. Here they are. Once you sign them, you can move in. The rent isn't due until the first of October."

Just as Curly finished signing and handed his pen to Shelly, his cell phone rang. "It's Chad again. I best take this. Be right back." He was only on the phone for a brief minute before he turned with a pale, serious face. Without explanation, he rushed out the door. "Shell, stay here with Nicole and Tim," he shouted as he raced out the door, letting it slam behind him.

* * *

Despite being told to hurry, Chad took his time wandering up and down every aisle in the small market. *Anything to just walk around and stretch! I would even welcome going to the outlets with Joelle right now! Sheesh! I'm so stiff from sitting!*

Realizing he couldn't justify dragging things out any longer, he made his way to the cashier to pay for his purchases. Standing in line, he noticed the huge guy in front of him, covered in tattoos.

That's some really interesting body art. His eyes lingered on one tattoo in particular. *Hmm, that one on his neck looks familiar. Where have I seen it before?*

After the man paid for his gas, Chad watched him walk out to a filthy white work van. As the vehicle pulled away, he couldn't help but notice one of the taillights was out but just shrugged.

Got bigger things than taillights to worry about. Maybe it'll come to me later where I saw that tattoo.

When he stepped to the counter, he was glad to see Eli, one of the boys he taught in Sunday School, was running the register. "Hey, man! That guy who just left. I thought I knew or had seen just about everyone who lives around here, but I don't recall ever seeing him before. Do you know him? I'd like to tell him his taillight is out before he gets pulled over."

"Nah, not really. He's been here a few times over the last several months. Always fills up the van and leaves without saying a word or buying anything else. He's really scary-looking and rude, so I just keep my mouth shut."

"Well, next time you see him, would you mind mentioning his taillight to him in case I don't see him?"

After finishing his conversation with Eli, Chad strode to his car, preoccupied with the artwork he'd seen. Realizing he had been gone much longer than planned, he pushed his speed up, and as he turned onto Hillview Road, he saw the same white van in front of him.

As soon as he saw it, the van braked and turned into the driveway of the house they were watching. Chad immediately grabbed his radio. "Nick. Hey, you see me, right? I know the driver of that van had to have seen me too. If I pull into Mrs. Angel's drive, he's gonna get suspicious. What should I do?"

"You're right. Don't pull in here. Go on to the next intersection, turn left, and park on that street. Then hoof it back over here. Leave the food and stuff in the car, and make sure you come in carefully from the back."

Once Chad was back in place, he caught Nick up on the tattoo he had seen. He tried describing it, but after making no progress, Nick pulled his notepad out and handed it to him. "Here, draw it. Hopefully, you're better at sketching than describing." When Chad was finished, Nick pulled his phone out and snapped a photo of the drawing before googling it. Then his expression darkened.

"Um, Chad, either you drew it wrong, or this is a huge coincidence. But I think we have trouble on our hands."

"What? What is it? I *know* I've seen it before." Nick turned his phone toward Chad, showing him the image on the screen. Chad's eyes widened. He gulped and said, "I best call Curly."

Chapter Thirty

Curly called Agent Tolley as he sped away from the farm, "Tolley, I need you and Willis to meet me at Mrs. Angel's house at 421 Hillview Road immediately." He paused. "Yes, I know you have your hands full with interviews from the hotline tips, but remember my brother, Chad?" At Tolley's grunt of recognition, Curly continued, "It seems he has inadvertently stumbled across a vital piece of information. I don't have all the details, and it will be much easier to explain in person. Ya'll just need to trust me and get to that address ASAP. I'm stopping by my place to grab my gun and change into my uniform. But since I live close to her place, I should still beat ya'll there."

Disconnecting the call, Curly turned into his place and quickly ran into his small apartment to change. *Wow, won't be long and we'll have a whole farm to live at! Thanks, Lord, for answering that prayer so quickly and in such a unique way! You never cease to amaze me.*

He was halfway out the door when he remembered his weapon. Groaning, he rushed back in and retrieved it from the small gun safe in their bedroom closet. After ensuring it was loaded, he sent Shelly a quick text:

> "Sorry I ran off so fast. Chad needs my help.
> Am meeting up with him and Nick. Will catch
> u up 2nite. Luvs ya."

Curly drove the short two miles over to Mrs. Angel's house, parking in front of Chad's car on Griffith Lane. He paused a moment in the car and surveyed his surroundings before getting out. Not finding anything amiss, he casually exited his vehicle and strolled toward Mayberry Street, the road behind Mrs. Angel's home.

As he approached, he easily spotted Nick and Chad behind the shed—just as they had said they would be. Curly shook his head when he saw Nick standing with his gun out while Chad peered intently across the street through the binoculars.

"Guys, Lieutenant Rogers here. Nick, do you really need a gun right now? Has something happened?"

Chagrined, Nick replied, "Nah, not really. But I didn't want to be caught off guard."

"I hear ya, but do me a favor and put that away before you hurt one of us. Now, Chad, start from the top and explain in detail what happened at the 7-11."

Nick took up the job of surveillance so Chad could focus on reporting to Curly all that had transpired. "Man, when Nick googled that image, imagine our surprise when we realized…"

Before he could finish, a shiny, black SUV raced into the driveway and squealed to a stop. Agents Willis and Tolley slammed their doors, and Willis began demanding answers before he had even shut his door. "Lieutenant Rogers, this better not be a huge rabbit trail you've sent us on. We have a table full of paperwork and interviews to conduct. We really don't have time to be gallivanting across the countryside."

Curly held up his hand to interrupt the lecture as he said,

"Before we do any explaining, please pull your vehicle over there behind those trees. Might as well wave a huge flag announcing federal agents are over here, and we really don't want whoever it is staying across the street to know we are here." Willis motioned for Tolley to do as Curly had said.

Once they were all back together, Curly continued, "As you know, I deputized my brother, Chad here, to help track down some meat that has gone missing from two of our elderly citizens. I will have him catch you up on all the details shortly, but he was just telling me about something he saw today, and I really need that information. So, Chad, please finish what you were saying."

Trying not to be intimidated that he had two federal agents standing and staring at him, he said, "Okay, so where was I? Oh yeah…so Nick had googled the tattoo I saw and imagine our surprise when we realized it is the symbol for Omega! And when I saw the tattooed man turn into the driveway we were watching, we figured we had best see what you think. I know that letter sent to that reporter was signed 'The Omega,' but I can't piece together how that would be connected to some stolen meat."

Tolley spoke up, "What's the big deal about stolen meat? And where did you see this Omega symbol?" Chad again reviewed his account to bring the agents up to speed. While he was doing that, Curly stepped away to think and devise a plan of action.

Hearing the agents were finished questioning Chad, Curly turned to Willis and said, "I propose that you, Tolley, and I walk over there. I'll knock on the front door while ya'll walk around. Let's see what we can find out."

"Hold on, Lieutenant. I know you're under loads of pressure from the governor to find these bombers, but if we find anything while on that property without a warrant, it won't be admissible in court. We'll stay here with your two deputies while you run back to your office and secure a search warrant. That way, if no one agrees to let us inside, we can still enter, and all that we find will be covered. You got a judge that will sign off on a warrant for us?"

Curly nodded. After giving Nick and Chad orders to follow the van if it left, he went back to his office to start the paperwork for the warrant. *Lord, please let this be the bomber! And please put a hedge of protection around my officers and agents as we serve this warrant later today.*

Chapter Thirty-one

Having the completed paperwork for the warrant in hand, Curly hurried over to the courthouse and Judge Cox's office, knowing he was his best bet for getting a signature. Despite calling ahead, the secretary still made him wait in her office. Unable to sit still, he started pacing from the small window overlooking Pilotview's downtown park to the hallway and back several times. Fighting to keep his frustration in check, he reviewed everything he knew—from the mall bombing to Chad seeing an Omega symbol on this guy's neck. He was still stymied at what on earth was happening and unable to see how it could all be connected.

Lost in thought, Curly about jumped out of his skin when the phone rang in the very quiet office. After a brief conversation, the secretary walked to the judge's door and opened it. "Your Honor will see you now."

Curly found himself biting his lip as he watched the elderly judge slowly peruse each item in the papers. *Come on! We don't have time for this! How long does it take to read two pages anyway? If this guy gets away because of this delay…*

Unable to hold back, Curly blurted out, "Your Honor? Is there anything missing? Any questions I can clear up? We're in a bit of a time crunch here. We really don't want this guy to disappear on us."

The judge leaned back in his worn leather chair, removed his glasses, and began chewing thoughtfully on the stem. He stared past Curly at the office door for a good two minutes before finally clearing his throat.

"Well, Lieutenant," he began slowly, "forgive me for slowing you down. I understand you are under a lot of pressure, and I want these bombings stopped as much as anyone. However, I also want to make sure we do everything correctly and have all our 'i's' dotted and our 't's' crossed. So, just give me a couple more minutes to re-read this. That is," the judge added, raising his eyebrows, "if that's alright with you?"

Curly gave a stiff nod, swallowing his frustration.

Finally, thirty minutes after entering the judge's chambers, Curly had the signed paperwork in hand. He immediately called Agent Willis as he quickly exited the courthouse. "Willis, I have the warrant. My ETA is ten minutes."

Once back at Mrs. Angel's house, Curly strapped on his vest while giving orders to Nick and Chad. "Ya'll are to stay here. Do not, under any circumstances, leave this post. Do you understand? Nick, if something goes sideways for the agents and myself, I want you to call in the state police. Don't try to be the knight in shining armor riding to our rescue. They are better equipped to deal with these things. Plus, I need you two over here securing the perimeter. If you see that van leave, then you can follow it, but call me immediately. Any questions? No, okay then, let's go do this."

With that, Curly then walked over to the two agents. "Ya'll ready? Let's go. I've wasted enough time getting this warrant."

The men climbed into the agents' SUV and drove across the street to the property in question. Overgrown hydrangea bushes bordered the edge of the property, making it difficult to see anything except the black, broken-up asphalt driveway. Once past the bushes, Curly scanned the area but didn't spot a van or, for that matter, any vehicles. *Hmm, maybe they've hidden it?*

Willis and Curly waited at the bottom of the cracked wooden steps to give Tolley time to move into position at the back door. Curly held the warrant in his left hand and all three men had their guns drawn down at their sides. Willis and Curly took positions on each side of the door as Willis used the flat side of his fist to bang on the door while Curly shouted out, "Police! We have a warrant to search these premises! Open up!"

Silence. Not even the faintest sound of movement inside. After thirty seconds, they repeated their announcement. When there was no response, Curly nodded at Willis, and he used his very large foot to kick the door open. The men rushed inside with guns drawn, shouting, "Police! Hands in the air!"

When they saw no one in sight on the bottom level, they radioed Tolley to enter from the back, and they began methodically clearing each room of the old two-story farmhouse. They found lots of debris and dirty dishes but no people.

Upstairs, they found one of the doors secured with a large, new-looking padlock. Willis gestured for Tolley to grab their bolt cutters from the SUV.

Tolley returned and snapped open the lock with no problems at all.

Once inside the locked room, they realized they had found the owner's security center. There were two large tables set up in an "L" shape along the walls with several computer monitors on them. Each monitor had four squares showing different camera feeds. Curly pointed at the first computer and said, "That's the front door that we just kicked in. I'd say these are of this property."

Willis nodded in agreement while Tolley started clicking through the images. "Hold up. Half of these images are of the house and the rooms that we just cleared. But where are these cameras?" He pointed to the screen. "They appear to be in a prison or something with cells and bars, but I don't see any people. Where is this?" Tolley asked as he continued playing with the controls.

Curly offered, "Well, my guess would be somewhere on this property since the other images are of this house. Our warrant covers everything on this property, so I say we go out back and take a good look around. I'm gonna call in my other officers to back us up 'cause it looks like a lot of wooded area back there."

After Curly had called Sheila at the station, instructing her to call everyone in to help, the three men exited through the back door. Guns drawn, they fanned out to begin looking for a structure that might house the prison seen in the footage.

Chapter Thirty-two

Kimmy inhaled slowly and carefully peered out from under the rags. Her heart beat wildly as she cautiously threw off the rags and stood. Fearful that one of the men may be lurking in one of the cells, she bolted from one end of the dungeon to the other, glancing into each cell before convincing herself she was alone.

I can't believe that he didn't see me under there! Thank you, Jesus, for blinding his eyes for me. I can't wait to tell Grandma June my own Daniel in the lions' den story!

She took a deep breath to steady her nerves. *Okay, Kimmy, don't get ahead of yourself here. You still need to get out of here and find a phone.*

She was very wary as she crept slowly up the stairs, her heart pounding hard with each step. When she reached the top and saw that the door was shut, her stomach dropped.

No way! I got away from that nutcase to be still locked down here? What am I going to do?

Frustrated and near tears, she slumped onto the top step, burying her face in her hands. After a few moments, she forced herself to look around for any overlooked clues or ways to escape. Nothing.

Her anger boiling over, she kicked the door out of extreme

desperation only to be shocked when the door slammed open. *You mean it was unlocked the whole time? You're such an idiot sometimes, Kimmy!*

When no one responded to all the noise, she climbed out. She found herself in a barn unlike anything she'd ever seen in Florida. It was thick with dust, and cobwebs draped over every surface.

She shrieked when she walked through a massive web, spotting the largest spider that she had ever seen in her life hanging on it. Frantically wiping the sticky strands off her face, she scrambled to the barn's opening and peeked around the edge. Tears sprang to her eyes when she discovered she was in the middle of the woods and not in a neighborhood as she had hoped.

Kimmy's entire life had been in the southern part of Florida surrounded by sand, palm trees, bright blue skies, no see-ums, snakes, and gators. Her extended family lived there too, so they rarely traveled far, even for vacations. As her dad always said, "Why go anywhere else when we live in paradise already?" He had finally taken them to the panhandle one year during Christmas break, but that was the farthest north Kimmy had ever been. Until now.

On the long ride up here in the van, she had glimpsed the "Welcome to North Carolina" sign through the windshield. Now that she found herself wandering through the North Carolina woods, she realized just how different this place was from Florida. She was amazed at all the different trees and how she couldn't see much because of all their leaves. At every new noise, she would jump, half expecting a hungry gator or, worse, Keno to appear. She finally remembered that alligators didn't live in the North Carolina woods, and she fervently hoped that Keno was far, far away.

Thinking of the man made her think of Chelsea and all the other girls. It broke her heart to think of all of them still under his control. Before she knew it, she was sobbing, tears streaming down her face as she prayed they would be rescued soon.

Being a Floridian, she was used to hot, humid summer days, but she desperately wished for a strong coastal breeze to cut through the oppressive, stagnant air. Within minutes, her clothing was plastered to her skin, and she was drenched in sweat.

Stepping over several fallen logs, she let out another shriek when she saw a small creek. She rushed over and immediately began scooping water to her mouth with cupped hands. This action brought to her mind another Bible lesson Grandma June had taught her about Gideon. *Yeah, learn from Gideon and keep your head up, girl. Never know what or who might be in these woods!*

The cool water refreshed her, and her mood improved even more when she discovered wild blueberry bushes along the creek. *Oh, yum! Thank you, Jesus!* After eating several handfuls, she fashioned a small pouch out of the tails of her shirt and filled it with as many berries as she could gather. Now that she had food and water, she felt a surge of hope and decided to stick close to the creek to see where it would lead her.

After walking for what seemed like miles, a new sound caught her attention—something besides the chirping of birds. She froze, her heart racing. *What is that? Be careful, girl. Don't want to find yourself in an even worse mess than before.* The closer she got to the noise the more she realized that it was music. She had never heard anything like it before in her life.

The creek led to a small clearing, where Kimmy spotted a bright red barn surrounded by all kinds of farm equipment. Behind the barn stood an enormous chicken coop, with at least fifteen chickens clucking and pecking around in the dirt.

On the left of the creek was a very nice-looking log cabin with a porch stretching the entire length of the house. Hanging baskets overflowed with flowers. On the mat in front of the door was a big brown dog lying on his back, snoring away.

Not wanting the dog to give her away, she stayed hidden among the trees, waiting to see if anyone was home. After a few minutes, the dog stood up and stretched as the screen door opened and a very tall man stepped out. He was older but didn't look as old as her granddad. Though the way he walked was just like her granddad who had been through several back surgeries. He stood there with a glass of water in one hand while ruffling his dog's head with the other. She watched as he walked to the porch banister. When he leaned against it, she noticed he had a gun tucked into the back of his shorts. Her heart raced as her instincts screamed danger.

Then, to her horror, he seemed to look straight at her.

"You going to come on out of there? Don't make this old man chase you down," the man called. "I've known you were here this entire time because my security system told me you were out here, not to mention you aren't that hard to see. If I was going to hurt you, I would've done so by now. Looks like you've had a rough time of it. I brought this water out here for you. Why don't you come out and get it?" The man didn't yell, but his voice easily carried to where she was crouching in the trees.

Kimmy gulped as it dawned on her that she didn't have much of a choice, especially knowing he had a gun. Still being cautious, she slowly stood and held her shaking hands up. Her voice quivered as she spoke. "Please, sir, please don't hurt me. I just need to use your phone."

When the man heard the fear in the young woman's voice, his entire demeanor changed from one of "get off my property" to one of a kind, grandfatherly type. *Well, what do I do with this mess? What in tarnation has happened to her? She can't be older than my granddaughter, Carrie.*

Chapter Thirty-three

Curly and the two agents felt a surge of relief as the rest of the Pilotview police force poured into the driveway just at the moment that they reached the back field. Waiting for his team to suit up, Curly pulled up the property's tax map on his tablet. After studying it for few minutes, he sent officers in pairs of two to do a thorough check of the grounds. He, Willis, and Tolley decided that they would start with the detached single-car garage behind the house. It didn't take them long to clear as it was unlocked and completely empty except for several oil stains on the floor. One fresh-looking stain indicated a vehicle of some kind had been parked there not long before they arrived.

The three men hustled to the three tobacco barns that were marked on the tax map as sitting deep in the woods at the edge of the property. After a quick perusal of all three barns to see if they could see a van, Curly turned to Willis. "Where could that van have gotten off to? Chad watched it turn in here, and they've been watching this place ever since and haven't seen anything leave, let alone a van. I was positive we were gonna find it in one of these barns."

Willis shrugged as he took a moment to look around. "I hear ya. It's a puzzle for sure. I don't know what to tell you, except maybe there's another driveway or path somewhere in these woods? The map says it's three acres, so they could've driven off through the woods."

"Hmm, maybe," Curly muttered. "Let me give my guys a heads up to keep their eyes open for any paths." After he completed that task, Curly called Sheila. "Put out a BOLO on a large, white Ford Transit van that has a taillight out. Be sure to mention that the driver is a suspect in the recent bombings, so proceed with utmost caution."

Once he got off the phone, the men began going through each barn carefully. This took much longer than the garage, as the barns were filled with old, rusty farm equipment covered in thick layers of dust and cobwebs. Even though the barn's front doors were long gone, light failed to penetrate the dark interior. It didn't take them long to develop a routine of moving equipment, pressing against walls, and inspecting every corner. The work was slow and tedious, but they were determined to see what they could discover if anything, and to uncover any clues hidden in the shadows.

After an hour of inspecting the first barn, they finally finished, so they took a fifteen-minute break to rehydrate with water and cool off in the shade of a large oak tree.

As soon as they entered the second barn, Curly held up a hand to stop everyone. "Hold on," he said, scanning the space. "This one doesn't look like the last one. Where are all the cobwebs? And look at this floor—dust all around the edges but not over there." He pointed his flashlight toward the back corner. "Tolley, I'll give you some light while you carefully go and see why it's so clean."

As Tolley cautiously made his way to the back corner, he

pointed out that there were a few footprints in the dust that were closer to the edge. "Looks like someone was tiptoeing in here."

When he reached the back corner, he knelt to examine the area before progressing any further. "Guys, you need to come see this too. I think there's a door of some kind in the floor here. But I don't see any kind of handle."

As he waited for the other two, he pulled a pair of latex gloves from his hip pocket and slipped them on. Carefully, he pressed against the rectangular area on the floor, testing for movement. He jumped back when a hidden door suddenly sprung open when he pushed on the front left corner. He stood up and aimed his flashlight into the dark opening, discovering a stairway descending into the shadows.

"Now there's something you don't see every day!" Tolley exclaimed. "A hidden stairway in a tobacco barn! And wow! Something down there stinks! I hope it's not rats. Please don't let there be rats. Anything but rats!"

Curly motioned for the other two to proceed him down the steps. When they reached the bottom step, the air grew thick, and darkness closed around them, broken only by the narrow beams of their flashlights. As their beams moved around in the dungeon, they froze in horror.

Dear Lord! What on earth is a prison cell doing down here in Pilotview? Curly wondered. Without saying a word, each man drifted off to begin inspecting the rows of grim, rusted cells.

"Hey Tolley," Willis called. "I found the source of the smell. Looks like someone was holding prisoners down here. They gave them buckets to use for toilets, and they haven't been emptied any time recently," Willis explained as he swatted at the flies buzzing around his face.

About halfway through their examination of the cells, Sheila called Curly on his cell phone. "Boss, I know ya have yer hands full, but I just got a mighty strange phone call from that new guy…a Mr. Alan Sadowski," she said. "He says that he just had a teenage girl stumble into his yard and that you need to get over there quick 'cause she has a crazy story for ya."

* * *

Alan set the glass of ice water on the porch step, then retreated to the far edge of the porch to sit in his white rocking chair. "Put your arms down. I'm not gonna shoot you. You've got to be pretty thirsty out in this heat, so go on. Get ya some water," he encouraged, gesturing toward the glass.

Kimmy slowly stepped toward the porch while looking around in all directions for any surprises. Right when she reached for the glass, a large dog galloped over, tail wagging furiously. Before she could react, the dog jumped up, rested its massive paws on her shoulders, and enthusiastically licked her face.

"Daisy! Stop that! That's no way to treat visitors. Let the girl have some water. Down, now!" Alan commanded from his chair while keeping a close eye on his unexpected guest.

Daisy's antics shattered the tension and made Kimmy giggle and relax. When the dog finally flopped onto the ground, Kimmy grabbed the water and gulped it down.

"You look like you have quite the story to tell," Alan said gently. "Why don't you take a seat either on the step or up here on a chair? I promise you're safe." He gestured toward the chair next to him. "My name is Alan Sadowski, but you can call me Al. And you've already met the queen of the castle, Daisy. I'm a retired state trooper from Texas, so there's nothing you can tell me that I haven't heard a million times before. Now, what's your name?"

"It's Kim. But most everyone calls me Kimmy," she replied as she sank onto the grass next to Daisy, who immediately rolled over for a belly rub.

"Well, Kimmy, mighty nice to meet you. Looks like Daisy has decided you are safe. I best warn you that once you begin petting her, she won't let you stop."

"Oh, I don't mind at all. She actually reminds me of Pixie, my golden retriever back home." At the mention of home, her face crumpled, and she broke down crying. Daisy immediately sat up, whimpering, and started licking Kimmy's face.

"Well, Kimmy, you mentioned needing a phone. I have one you are welcome to use on one condition. Before I give you the phone, you need to tell me what has you so scared."

Chapter Thirty-four

"Mom, I'm sorry! I'm so very sorry," Kimmy sobbed into the phone. "I should've listened to you and Dad. If only I had…" Sobbing, Kimmy was unable to continue as she was overcome with emotion at the sound of her mother's reassuring voice.

"Kimmy, please stop apologizing! Your dad and I are just so thankful that you're okay! We've been imagining so many horrible things and have had everyone at church praying for you. When we get there, you can tell us all that happened, but for now, we just need Mr. Sadowski's address. Your dad and I will be on the first available flight that we can get." Kimmy relayed the needed information to her mom, who promised to call with their flight plans. "Just hang in there, sweetheart. We love you," her mom said before she ended the call.

Alan approached the kitchen and stopped when he saw Kimmy with her head buried in her arms on the table, her shoulders shaking with sobs. Giving her some space and time to get it all out, he quietly walked to the stove to make omelets from his supply of fresh eggs that he had gathered up that morning.

Kimmy lifted her head and said, "Mmm, something smells amazing! After weeks of eating pig slop, that's really making me hungry." She gave Daisy another rub behind her collar and added,

"Thank you for letting me call my mom. She said that they'll call back to tell me their flight plans." She inhaled deeply. "Seriously, something smells really good!"

Alan had just slid the second omelet onto the plate, so he carried them into the dining area. "Figured you could use something warm to eat," he said, handing one of the plates to Kimmy. After passing out napkins, forks, and condiments, Alan encouraged her to dig in.

When Kimmy put the first bite into her mouth, she gasped, "Oh, wow! This is delicious. This is possibly the best omelet that I've ever had!"

Alan chuckled. "Yeah, fresh eggs taste so much better than store-bought ones. If you want a second omelet, just let me know. I'd be glad to whip you up another one. I've got plenty of eggs in there. I've even got some picante sauce to add to it. That's how us Texans eat them."

He leaned back against his seat. "The police should be here any minute, though, so you just eat and enjoy. And ignore Daisy. Despite her pitiful face, she just had her lunch. Right girl?"

Hearing her name, Daisy sniffed the air before walking off and plopping down in front of her crate with an exaggerated huff.

As Alan loaded the dishwasher with their dirty dishes, Daisy began barking and bolted to the front door. Alan wiped his hands on the dish towel and tucked his gun into the back of his shorts again as he approached the door. Peeking out, he saw Curly getting out of his police cruiser.

Alan turned and told Kimmy, "Just stay there on the couch. I'll be back shortly." He turned to the dog. "Daisy, stay." He then went out to greet Curly. After explaining to Curly how he found Kimmy hiding on his property, he invited the lieutenant into the house.

Curly nodded but held up a hand. "Well, Alan, I sure do appreciate you calling us. Before we head inside, would you mind handing me your handgun that I see you've got tucked in your waistband? I'll give it back to you when I leave."

After handing his gun over, Alan led Curly inside. Once everyone was seated with glasses of ice water, Curly pulled out his voice recorder, a notepad, and a pen. He leaned back in the dark, brown recliner as he began. Giving Kimmy a reassuring look, he reached out to rub Daisy's ears as he started his interview. "Kimmy, I'm Lieutenant Greg Rogers. Before we start, please tell me your full name, birthdate, and where you are from."

"I'm Kimberly Ann Thornberry. My birthday is November 17th, 2001, and I'm from Fort Lauderdale, Florida," she replied softly as she pulled her legs up under her on the couch. Daisy, sensing her unease, hopped up next to her and rested her head on Kimmy's lap. When Kimmy began rubbing her belly, Daisy settled in for a good nap.

"Fort Lauderdale, huh? You're a long ways from home." He leaned forward slightly. "I'm sure you would rather not relive what you've been through, but it's important for me to get all the details from you while things are still fresh in your mind. Can you tell me how you got from Florida to Pilotview, North Carolina?"

"Well, Lieutenant Rogers, it's pretty stupid actually. I'm actually embarrassed and ashamed at how foolish I was," Kimmy answered as her fingers played with Daisy's ears.

"Trust me, Kimberly, I've been doing this long enough that nothing surprises me anymore. So, relax, breathe, and start at the beginning," he encouraged.

Taking a deep breath and letting it out, she began. "Okay, so I work at a place called Flamingo Gardens in Davie, Florida, which is near Fort Lauderdale. There was this cute guy, well, I used to think he was cute. Anyway, there was this cute guy, Keno, who rode my tram one day and then was at the grill when I took my lunch break. We hit it off and began chatting. He asked me out, and I agreed."

Her voice faltered for a moment, then she continued. "We planned to meet up at a place called El Camino, which is in downtown Fort Lauderdale. When I told my mom about the date, she warned me to take a friend along, but I figured I'd be safe because I was meeting him there at the restaurant. That way, I could leave if things didn't look right or went bad.

"So, when I got to the restaurant, Keno was already sitting at the table and had ordered two sodas for us. He said that he remembered that I drank Mountain Dew at lunch, so he went ahead and ordered a glass of it for me."

She paused, then suddenly hit herself on the head. "Man, how stupid! I *know* better! That must be when he drugged me because that's the last thing that I remember before waking up sick in the hotel room. I was so excited to be going out with such a good-looking guy that I completely forgot all those lectures from my dad about never accepting any open drinks from a guy." At the thought of her dad, tears started streaming down her face again. She frantically wiped at the tears with her sleeve, her shoulders trembling as Daisy shifted in closer, nuzzling against her side in comfort.

Curly cleared his throat and said, "Kimberly, listen to me—you didn't do this. This guy, Keno, is the guilty one, not you. Quit beating yourself up over it. And I'm fairly sure that your mom and dad aren't gonna be mad at you over this. Right now, the best thing you can do is focus on helping me catch him for doing this to you. Take a second and just breathe."

Alan leaned over and handed her a box of tissues. After dabbing her tears, Kimmy took a huge breath and picked up her story again. "Okay, so, I woke up sick as a dog. Excuse me, Daisy. Sick on my stomach in a regular hotel room. I was chained to the wall. There was another girl in the room with me, Chelsea. She was also chained to the wall. Then Keno and another guy, Murray, came and loaded us up into a van."

Curly's eyes narrowed. "A van? What kind of van?"

"Um, it was one of those work vans. Dirty, didn't have any windows in the back. There were a bunch of other girls around my age already in the back. As the two of us were getting in, I noticed the hotel was on the beach in Hollywood, Florida. My family goes to that beach all the time, so I recognized it right away. After they put us in the van, they zip-tied our wrists and ankles like the other girls."

Curly scribbled in his notepad. "That's about a twelve- or thirteen-hour drive from here, I believe. How did these guys manage to control this many women when they stopped for gas or at the rest stops? Did they even stop to let you use the restroom?" Curly inquired.

"Yeah, they did."

"That had to be pretty difficult for them to manage without anyone else noticing ya'll," Curly pressed.

Kimmy shook her head. "Oh, he stopped at houses out in the country. He warned us at the start that they owned properties on the way, so we wouldn't be able to run away. And he threatened to shoot us if we made a scene at the gas stations." Kimmy paused, taking a couple of gulps of water before continuing. "Where I sat in the back, I could see out the front window. Thank goodness because I get bad car sickness when I can't see. Anyway, I remember seeing the 'Welcome to North Carolina' sign. Not long after that, he took the King-Tobaccoville exit. Then he drove through the countryside a bit before he pulled into the place I just escaped from."

Chapter Thirty-five

Curly's phone rang, interrupting Kimmy's account of how she had hidden in a pile of rags to escape.

"It's Sheila from the station," he said before stepping into the next room to take the call. Closing the door behind him, he pressed the phone to his ear. "Yeah, Sheila, what's up?" he asked, keeping his voice down so he wouldn't be heard.

"Curly, seems the boys need ya to go back over to Hillview Drive. One of them has found something they think ya need to see," Sheila told him before popping a bubble with her gum.

Curly sighed. "Tell them it will be at least another hour or two before I am finished up here and can get back over there. I really need to finish taking this statement first."

"Um, okay. You're the boss, but they said to tell ya it was mighty important."

"Hold on. Let me call you right back." Curly ended the call and walked back into Alan's den. "Alan, it looks like I'm needed back at the other property. Normally, I would have one of my female officers take Kimmy into protective custody, but right now, I don't have any officers, male or female, available for anything. They're all quite busy at the moment. So, I had Sheila check you out back when Pastor first told me about you, and I know that you're a retired state trooper from Texas. By any chance, would I be able to leave Kimmy here in your care? Just until I can get back to finish her statement?"

Alan leaned forward in his recliner, propping his elbows on his knees as he hung his hands between his legs. A grin spread across his face, and he let out a soft chuckle. "Well, Lieutenant, that's going to be a tad bit difficult to do seeing as how you have my gun."

Curly paused, then broke into a huge smile. "Hey, no hard feelings! I don't like anyone having a weapon unless they are an officer of the law. And like I believe this is your only weapon on this property. Here. You can have it back." Alan chuckled again as Curly handed the gun back to him.

"Now repeat after me…" Once Curly had Alan deputized, he explained to Kimmy how vital it was for her to stay there with Alan. He then gave his card to both of them as he walked out to his vehicle. "My number's on there. Call me if you need me."

Driving back over to Hillview Drive, Curly mentally reviewed everything he had just heard. *Lord, sure sounds like we have a human trafficking ring right here in little ole' Pilotview!* Curly gripped the steering wheel tighter. *This stuff just makes me sick. Thank you for showing Kimmy a way of escape, but, Lord, I can't help but worry about all those other girls who didn't get away.*

Curly let out a heavy sigh. *Please, please show me something so I can find them before it's too late. And on top of this, I need to find those bombers! How on earth do I have human traffickers AND bombers in Pilotview?* He rubbed his temples. *Something just isn't adding up here. Too many strange coincidences— and I don't believe in coincidences.*

By the time he finished praying, he was parking his car. He slammed the door and then strode over to the agents who were standing in the drive waiting on him. "Hey, guys. Sheila tells me that I'm needed here. What's up?"

"Just follow us," Willis replied, heading toward the woods in the back of the property. As they pushed deeper into the thick woods, Curly began hearing his officers' voices; he also noticed that they were coming around the back side of the property to behind the tobacco barns. As they drew nearer, he could see most of his police force was walking carefully around, examining the ground.

"Again, what's up?" Curly asked Willis.

"One of your guys was out surveying the property, looking for another driveway, and stumbled upon this well-hidden path," Willis explained, pointing to a nearly invisible break in the dense woods. "If you notice, you can't even see it from here. They've allowed the grass to grow up high along both sides of that path, like they're trying to camouflage it. Your guy; what was his name again, Tolley?"

"Officer Vesper, I believe," Tolley answered.

"Yeah, your guy, Officer Vesper, literally stumbled onto it. He was just walking along when he noticed what looked like two stripes in the grass like someone had driven repeatedly on it. He called it into your gal back at the station, and here we are," Willis said as he used his long arm to wave in the direction of the path and all the officers walking around.

Tolley stood with his hands on his hips as he also looked around. "Lieutenant, I do believe this is why no one saw that van leave here. Look at how that path leads up to the back of that tobacco barn where we found that dungeon."

Curly nodded in agreement, motioning for the group to follow as he headed toward the path. After inspecting how the path was exactly as they had described, he then walked over to the back of the barn to begin examining it.

"Look here, guys!" he called out, crouching near a section of the barn wall. "Isn't this a door here? It's been very well-hidden. I bet they had the girls exit through here before loading them into the van. Then they could just drive out from here without being seen.

"Let me check something out." Curly pulled the tax map back up on his tablet and pointed at it as he showed the agents. "Yeah, that's what I figured. See here? This land backs up to Coon Hollow Road. From there, they could turn onto Perch and then onto Highway 52. Then it's just a short drive to the interstate. They're probably long gone by now. Hopefully, along with what Kimmy just gave us, our guys will find something in the house or dungeon to point us to them."

"Wait. Back up. You have a witness? Where is this witness? We need to talk to them," Willis said as he stared at Curly.

"The witness is somewhere safe. I'll set something up once we have everything finished up here."

Chapter Thirty-six

"Tuck, after you finish taping up this box, please label it 'Office Supplies'." Shelly groaned as she slowly stood, arching her back as she stretched. "I think all we have left to pack is our clothes and the pantry stuff. We should be ready for the big move here shortly. Sheesh, between the packing, Chad's graduation, and your tournament this weekend, it's going to be crazy around here."

She paused, a slight smile creeping onto her face. "Why don't we go take a break with some lemonade and cookies?" She went into the kitchen and poured some cold lemonade into the paper cups they were using for their glasses. She then offered the package of chocolate chip cookies to Tucker to carry for her. "Let's go out back so Max can run around some."

Once they were seated, Max promptly ran to pick up his favorite tennis ball. He bounded over to Tucker and dropped it at his feet while prancing around and swishing his tail back and forth in anticipation. Tucker laughed as he began their daily game of fetch.

Shelly leaned back and enjoyed watching the dog and boy play until Max finally had enough and collapsed under Tucker's chair. She then cleared her throat while she turned to Tucker and said, "Tuck, Curly and I have been wanting to talk to you for a few days now, but with all that's going on in town, there just hasn't been a good chance…"

Tucker looked over at her as he interrupted, "What did I do? Am I in trouble? I ain't done nothing wrong."

"No, no…nothing like that. It just…well, we've both noticed that you've seemed a tad bit down lately. Is everything okay? Are you upset about moving?"

"Huh, nah! I done told ya I'm glad we're movin' to Nicole's old place. Nothin' like that is botherin' me." Tucker shrugged and hung his head after he took another gulp of lemonade.

"Well, if it's not that, then what is bothering you?"

"I'm fine," he replied so quietly that she almost couldn't hear him.

"Tuck, come on now. It's me. We've been through so much together, and I couldn't love you more, even if I had given birth to you. I know something's got you upset. I can feel it. Curly even noticed as well. We're a bit worried about you," she paused to see if he would explain, but when the silence just stretched on, she reached over and rubbed his shoulder. "Whatever it is, just remember that you are not alone in it. You can talk to me or Curly about anything. You know that, right?" After he jerked his head in a quick nod, she continued, "Well, Tuck…"

"Mama Shelly, it's just…it's just that all this bad stuff keeps happening to everyone I love. First, Mom and Dad died, and then you were almost dead in the hospital. And then Curly! I know you're jest gonna say I need to keep trustin' God, but I jest wish…I jest…" Tucker started sobbing and couldn't finish his sentence. Before Shelly could even speak, he jumped up and ran inside.

Dear Jesus, that boy's really struggling! What do I say? What do I do? Please give me and Curly wisdom to guide him through this. Shelly paused her prayer to take another sip of lemonade and gasped when she looked at her watch. *Yikes! We've got to get a move on. We're gonna be late!*

She commanded Max to heel as they went inside and threw away their cups and the empty cookie package. "Tuck! We need to get moving! I didn't realize it was so late. You're supposed to be on the field in thirty minutes!" she yelled as she walked back to check on him. Her heart broke when she opened his door to find him lying on his bed with his back to the door.

"I'm not goin'."

"What do you mean? This weekend is the start of the tournament that you've been so excited about. You really need to be at practice if you expect to play this weekend. Plus, your team needs you," she encouraged as she sat at the end of his bed and rubbed his leg. Max trotted in and jumped up next to him. He circled a couple of times before plopping down next to Tucker with his head on his leg.

"Mama Shelly, I just don't feel like it. They'll be fine without me," he mumbled in reply.

"Well, Tuck, there's always going to be days where you don't feel like doing something, but you still must do it anyways. Listen, I'm going to put my foot down. You'll feel better once you are out there playing and are around the other guys."

"So, are you sayin' I have to?" he asked as he turned to look at her.

"Yep, that's what I'm saying. So, go wash your face and grab your bag. It's ready for you in the laundry room. I'll meet you in the car in five minutes or less. Now, let's go!"

Tucker sighed loudly but got up and stomped to the bathroom without saying a word. Seeing he was moving, she went and filled the cooler with drinks and snacks, then made sure Max's water and food bowls were topped off. After glancing around to confirm she had everything, she went out to the car to wait for her reluctant son.

As she sat waiting, she shot off a quick text to Curly:

"Hey, hon! Had a short talk with Tuck. Will catch u up after practice. Luv ya."

Just a few seconds later, her phone pinged with his reply:

"Good. I will be home eventually. Got a mess on my hands. Tell Tuck I'm proud of him."

Chapter Thirty-seven

"Murray! You idiot! Did you even think to count the merchandise? We are one short!" Keno smacked Murray on the side of the head as they drove east on Interstate 40 toward Wilmington.

Murray jerked as he replied, "There's no way I missed any one of those girls! You or Marshall counted wrong. Count again."

"Don't go blaming Marshall; his only job was to babysit the girls. It's just the two of us from here on out as he's lying low, keeping his cover as the school janitor." Keno pounded the steering wheel in frustration. "I've already counted twice. The boss will kill us if even one girl is missing."

He glanced into the rear-view mirror and growled, "I don't see that girl I picked up from Flamingo Gardens—Kimmy? How did you let her escape? She could blow our whole operation wide open."

"Me? How is this all my fault? You're the one who was in such a rush that you wouldn't even give me time to clean out the stalls and do our standard sterilization."

"Enough! We either need to find her immediately or replace her with another girl before we reach Wilmington. Otherwise, we're both dead. I just bet she's still in one of the stalls and was just too weak to stand up. Turn here, and let's circle back."

Meanwhile, at Alan's house, Kimmy had showered and changed into a pair of sweatpants and a t-shirt his daughter had left behind after her last visit. Kimmy felt better after the agents arrived with Curly. Once the agents were seated, she told them about how she had managed to hide in a pile of nasty rags after the girl unlocked their handcuffs off them.

Willis grunted and shook his head. "You are one very lucky young lady."

Kimmy gave a small smile and cleared her throat as she struggled not to cry. "Well, sir, you could say that, sure. But I had been praying really hard, and I believe that God showed me what to do so that I could get free and then be able to show you all something that would lead you to rescue the rest of the girls. We've just got to stop them before they sell them. It's just crazy!"

"And we will. The best help you can give us is to go over every word and thing you saw or heard while with them. Anything at all. No detail is too small. It sounds to us like Pilotview is a station along a human trafficking route from Fort Lauderdale to Wilmington and then to anywhere in the world.

"Unfortunately." Willis continued. "What happened to you, Kimmy, is very common. A good-looking young man will flirt with a young college-age girl and arrange for a date. Sometime after they meet, she will be kidnapped. Most of the time, no one ever sees them again."

Willis' eyes became serious. "They aren't going to be happy that you got away. You represent an awful lot of money to them, so we need you to stick close to Alan here until we get this whole thing figured out or can find you some protection. Now, Tolley is pretty decent at sketching. Would you be able to describe these men, Keno and Murray, to him? It will be a huge help in tracking them down."

* * *

As they approached Hillview Drive, Keno had Murray take the back road, which was basically a farming path. About a mile from their destination, Keno ordered him to pull over and park the van behind a dilapidated lean-to shed. The structure, once used for storing farming equipment, was now piled high with rusted-out junk.

Keno ordered Murray, his voice sharp and impatient. "Stay with the girls and the van," he barked. "And don't mess this up." Without waiting for a reply, he took off at a fast clip towards the direction of the barn, cursing Murray the whole way.

As he drew closer to the barn, Keno slowed, his senses heightened. Moving, he began to cautiously advance from tree to tree and then came to a complete stop as he heard the murmur of voices. He strained to listen, his heart pounding in his chest. *Probably just hunters,* he thought, as his fingers tightened around the gun in his pocket.

"Quit yer messing around, Frank! The Lieutenant told us to keep our eyes and ears open as we watch the perimeter. I don't think throwing rocks at squirrels is what he meant, and you know how bad I need this job. Don't go screwing it up for me."

"Oh quit yer belly achin'. Ain't nothin' gonna happen out here. That's why he assigned us this here spot. He knew nothin' good would happen here. Did ya hear Jerry and Pete saying how there was a girl that escaped and showed up at that new fella's place?" Frank asked as he threw another rock at another squirrel up in the oak tree above their heads.

"A girl escaped? They're just messin' with ya! What the tarnation are ya talkin' about?"

"Seriously, man! Seems there is this girl from down in Florida that jest walked into that dude's yard and claimed she had been kidnapped. Crazy, huh? Here in little ole Pilotview, NC!"

Keno had heard enough. He stepped out from behind the tree while pointing a handgun at the two men. "Sounds very interesting to me. Now, this is how this will go if you two want to ever see your families again. Throw your guns down on the ground. Don't try anything funny." When they had obeyed, he continued, "Now, lie down, hands behind your heads. One of you start talking and tell me where this girl is. If you don't start talking fast, I'll start with shooting out your knees, then your shoulders, then…well, you get the idea. And, if you scream? You die. Now, where is she? Start talking now!"

Frank jumped up to his feet and tried to make a run for the woods while desperately trying to push the button on his shoulder radio to call for help. Keno didn't even blink as he shot him in the back. "I am not playing games. Now, what's your name?"

After gulping and stammering for a few seconds, the man finally answered, "Carmine."

"Okay, Carmine, talk fast before your friends spoil the party. Where is she? Now that it's just the two of us, I can give you my undivided attention. You decide whether this will be easy or hard."

"I'll tell ya! I'll tell ya! Just don't kill me, please! I have kids at home, man!" Between sobs, Carmine quickly gave Keno the directions to Alan's neighboring farm. Then, working quickly, Keno stripped him down, tied and gagged Carmine to a tree.

"See, when you cooperate, I'm not such a bad guy," he said as he lightly smacked him on the side of the face. It took him a little over an hour to reach Alan's place, weaving silently through the woods. Every movement calculated as he blended seamlessly into the surroundings, determined to avoid detection by the cops looking for him and to get his hands on that valuable girl.

* * *

As the agents talked with Kimmy, Curly and Alan stepped into the kitchen to grab a cup of coffee and started talking over all that had been happening around Pilotview. Curly ran his hands through his curly hair in frustration. "Al, I just know all of this must be connected. There's just no way that our little town has two bombings, terrorist threats, human traffickers, and meat thieves all in one week. It just *has* to be, but I can't make the pieces fit. My brain must be fried from this concussion."

Alan leaned his tall body against the kitchen counter and took a sip of the hot coffee before answering. "You know, Curly, he began. "I've had some time to just sit on my porch out here and think about this. Here's my idea: what do human traffickers need for their 'merchandise'? Food. Maybe that's the source of your meat thief right there."

Curly raised an eyebrow as Alan continued. "And didn't the

first bomb happen right after Jed came into your office filing his complaint about the missing meat? Maybe whoever's behind all this thought that Jed was onto them and used the bombs as distractions to get their shipment through." Alan shrugged and took another sip. "Just a thought."

Curly stared at his coffee for a moment, then snapped his finger and pointed at Alan. "A really *good* thought! Now, why didn't I think of any of that?"

"Well, give yourself a break. You are recovering from a concussion, and your wife was in the hospital…" Before he could finish the sentence, his alarm started squealing. "Everyone, quick! We have an intruder! Follow me!"

Chapter Thirty-eight

Murray finished giving each girl a swallow of water before securing the van doors with the padlock. Stretching his arms, he checked his phone again to see if Keno had texted. Seeing that there were still no new texts, he decided to call his wife back in Florida.

"Hey, Baby. I know I told you Friday, but this job is taking a little longer. We ran into some construction in Virginia, so I probably won't be home until Monday. How's Junior doing?" As they chatted, Murray froze at the sharp crack of a gunshot echoing through the woods. "Um, baby, that's great," he said quickly, his voice faltering. "Yeah, uh, so that's the boss. I've gotta run. I'll call you later. Love ya."

Hanging up, he stared toward the direction of the sound, his mind racing. *A gun shot! Surely Keno didn't shoot her! Maybe he's just scaring her. Oh man. What's going on? Maybe I should text him. But he said never text him. But it's been an hour already.*

"Hey, K, you okay? I heard a shot."

Murray's fingers trembled as he hit send. As he waited for a reply, he got up and started pacing around the van. Then he froze when he heard dogs barking off in the distance. *Dogs? Oh man. We are screwed! Why isn't he answering me? Come on, Keno, answer me!*

Then, a couple of minutes later, a helicopter swooped overhead, its spotlight scanning in the direction of the barn. Murray's breath hitched, and his gut twisted with a sick realization. Keno must be dead. *They got him. That's it. I'm out of here. I'm not dying today.*

Murray sent one more text:

> "K, pretty sure you are dead, but if not, I'm
> headed to W. Catch ya there."

He then jumped into the van and drove back east towards Wilmington.

* * *

"What's up, Al?" Agent Willis demanded.

"We have an intruder that set off my perimeter alarms. I'm now looking at my cameras to see where he is. Yes, here he is. Okay, I have a secure room. Which one of you is staying with Kimmy?"

"Al, I'm the agent and will be the one giving the orders," Willis said while Alan continued scanning the cameras on his tablet.

Alan chuckled as he replied, "Yeah, that's how it works on paper, but you're on my property and what I say goes here. Tolley, you take Kimmy and Daisy to the safe room down in the basement. Daisy is trained to protect and guard. If anyone gets near you two, just say a-t-t-a-c-k. She'll give her life for you. The code to the room is 6921 and there are guns and food in there. Go now! Daisy, go, guard. Curly, Willis, with me."

Alan led the two men into his bedroom walk-in closet where he had stored several tactical vests and a large gun safe. Once the men were outfitted, they once again reviewed the cameras on the tablet and saw that the intruder hadn't moved. "Good, he's not stupid. I hate stupid criminals. You two go out back while I step out front. He knows we see him."

Alan cocked his twelve-gauge shotgun and stepped out onto his front deck while aiming it directly at the tree where he knew Keno was hiding. "You there. I know you are there. You know I can see your sorry butt. I've got two officers coming behind you. So, I'm going to give you to the count of three to throw out your gun and come out with your hands up."

When Keno spotted the cameras in the tree, he froze, his pulse racing. *Stay calm. See if there's a reaction.* As soon as the front door began opening, he started walking backwards as quickly and carefully as he could. Once he reached the section he knew was clear of any surveillance, he broke out into a full-out sprint back to where he had left the two cops.

"You! You failed to mention there were cameras!" Keno punched him in the side of the head out of frustration. "Now, I'm going to remove the gag, and you're going to tell me every little thing that you know about this man and his property. Understand?"

"I swear! I swear! I didn't know! He just moved to town not too long ago. I don't even know the man. I don't know anything. There's nothing to tell you. Please. Please don't kill me. I've got a family."

Keno looked around. "Okay. I guess I believe you. In fact, I'm out of here. It's just too much trouble for one dumb broad. You can go ahead and yell your stupid head off all you want. This has turned out to be way too much work. Adios!" At that, Keno turned and ran off into the woods in the opposite direction until he was out of sight of the police officer; then, he circled back around and waited. Sure enough, the cop started hollering and crying his head off. *That should do it.*

When no one came out from behind the tree, Alan waited for Curly and Willis to circle around before he dropped his shotgun and checked his cameras. "We're clear. He's gone. You can tell Tolley to come on out." Before Willis had even finished the text to Tolley, they heard someone shouting for help. Alan checked his cameras and saw that all was still secure.

Curly said, "I've got to see what that is all about. Could be one of my men. I'll be right back."

"No way, Lieutenant, you don't go by yourself. Could be a trap. We will go with you, right, Al?" Willis turned and looked at Alan as Curly stopped at the bottom of the steps.

"I agree. Willis, let Tolley know that I've just armed my security and cameras. Let's go," Alan said as he led the men down a well-hidden path on the side of the property.

Keno watched as the three men quickly found one dead officer and the other one tied to the tree. *That should keep them busy for a little while. I'm going to have to do something about those cameras. Maybe Temu can help me out from Fort Lauderdale. I'll give him a call when I get there.*

Keno immediately started back towards Alan's place, but this time, he made sure to stay on the edge of the property until Temu could instruct him on how to disable the security or electricity.

Meanwhile, Murray was clueless that his broken taillight had attracted the attention of a North Carolina State Trooper as he had been stuck in construction around Raleigh. When the trooper called it in, his commander informed him that there was a statewide manhunt for a van with a broken taillight. He was to hang back and follow until further orders were given.

Chapter Thirty-nine

"Officer down! I repeat, officer down! Another officer is requiring medical assistance in sector twelve-b. Get an ambulance back here STAT!" After Curly finished getting his officers moving, he helped Carmine back into his uniform while visually assessing his injuries. As Curly questioned him about what had happened, Willis took Alan and started putting up crime scene tape and getting a perimeter in place before everyone trampled all over the evidence.

"Carmine, can you tell me what happened? Who did this to you?" Curly crouched beside the injured officer, his jaw tight as he fought to keep his anger in check at losing Frank . *I really don't want to tell Frank's mama he is gone. Please let us get something worthwhile out of this, Lord. Please!*

"Sir, Frank and I, we were back here jest like we was told to be. Looking for any bad guys or white vans. And, Frank, well, sir, you know how he is, um, I mean, was. He liked to goof off some. And he started throwing rocks at the squirrels, trying to scare them all 'cuz we were bored out of our minds. I had to tell him to knock it off and pay attention. Next thing I know, this dude is standing right there in front of us with a gun pointed at us!" Carmine was getting all worked up again, just remembering it and started breathing faster and faster.

"Slow down, son, slow down," Curly said. "Look, I see the EMT's coming this way. Just take in a nice deep breath and let it out nice and slow. Good. Now another one. That's it." As the EMT approached, Curly gave Carmine a reassuring nod. "They'll take good care of you. I'll be back when they're done looking you over."

Straightening up, Curly strode over to Alan and Willis. "Thoughts?"

Alan grunted and said, "Yeah, why did he let Carmine live? These guys don't usually leave anyone living behind. So why did he leave him alive? You need to find the answer to that question. And while you're at it, find out exactly what Frank and Carmine were talking about out here that this guy might have overheard and everything Carmine told him. It looks like he got worked over pretty good, so chances are he probably told him everything he knew. But again, the big question is: why is Carmine alive?"

Willis nodded; his brow furrowed. "Yep, I was wondering the same thing and would've said it was a trap, but nothing happened."

Alan's eyes widened. "Trap! Not here! We're fools. This is just a diversion! Hurry, Curly! Find out whatever you can from Carmine because I've got a bad feeling that this was just a ploy to draw us away from the house. He must really want Kimmy bad!" Alan urged as he checked his phone to make sure all was still secure at the house.

Curly rushed over to Carmine, interrupting the EMT's examination. "Carmine, there's no time. Did you and Frank discuss the kidnapped girl at all?"

"Well, sure we did. But jest that she got away and made it over to Al's place, next place over to this one."

"Did this guy overhear that?"

"He must have because he asked a bunch of questions. In fact, that's why he punched me. Because I didn't tell him about the cameras on Al's property. But I told him that I didn't know about no cameras or anything about his place at all."

"Carmine, why did he kill Frank and not you?"

"Man, Frank jest got scared and jumped up and started to run for it. That crazy dude just shot him in the back without even blinking. If he would've just kept still, he would still be alive! It's weird though."

"What's weird?"

"Well, at first, the guy gagged me and left for a long time. Then he came back and told me the girl was too much trouble, and he was out of here. Then he removed the gag and left. I guess he didn't care if I screamed or not."

"Thanks, Carmine. We'll be back to go over your statement again in more detail later. Now just take it easy." Curly ran back over to Willis and Alan.

"You nailed it, Alan. He tried a misdirection with Carmine by saying the girl is too much trouble. I believe he's gone back to your place."

"I've been checking my system, and everything is still secure."

Willis held up his hand. "This time, we do things my way. I'm calling in a SWAT team. I've already alerted Agent Tolley to be on high alert. The three of us need to head back over there and just observe before the SWAT team arrives, then we'll assist them. If we observe any distress, then we can step in. Understand?"

Alan shrugged. "I don't like it, but I understand. As of right now, my cameras still show everything as secure."

"Good," Willis replied. "Let's go."

* * *

Keno sat on the edge of the road, waiting for his tech guy, Temu, in Fort Lauderdale to work his magic and hack into the security system to disable it. While he waited, he decided it was time to deal with Murray.

"I told you to wait for me and you up and leave me stranded? I swear, Murray, the next time I see you, you're as good as dead to me!" Keno seethed.

"Keno! You're alive!" Murray yelled through the phone. "Listen man, I really thought you were dead. I heard a gunshot and then dogs barking. Then this helicopter came swooping over. I had to keep our merchandise safe!"

"Where. Are. You?"

"Um, I'm somewhere on the other side of Raleigh. I'm getting ready to make a stop at our place near here so the girls can use the restroom, get some water and food."

"Okay now, this time listen carefully. You wait for me there until I get there with Kimmy. Do I make myself clear? Do. Not. Leave. Until. I. Get. There. And whatever you do, make sure that you aren't followed. I'm not there to keep an eye on your tail."

"Keno, you worry too much. No one is following me. We've

been stuck in a lot of construction and then rush-hour traffic. It's just now opening up. Man, I'm so glad you're not dead! I really thought you were a goner, dude."

"Yeah, yeah. Later." Keno disconnected the call with a sharp tap and muttered, "Idiot," under his breath. He looked for a text from Temu, but nothing had come through. Frustrated, he gave him a call.

"Come on, man," Keno hissed when Temu answered. "I don't have much time here. There's cops everywhere."

"I'm working on it. This dude's got heavy encryption on it, but I'm almost through. In the meantime, I'm sending you the layout of the house." Keno's phone pinged. "Looks like there might be a space in the basement with way more wiring than a normal house would need. Could be a safe room."

"Finally! Someone who's doing what they're being paid to do. Now, how much longer until these cameras are down?"

"Just three more seconds. I have the cameras in a loop so it looks like everything is good to him. However, I'm having difficulty shutting down that safe room. Okay, you're clear. Go. Will text when the room is open."

"I owe you one, Temu." Keno took off at a sprint for the back of the house, constantly looking for that dog he'd spotted earlier. Reaching the back door with no issues, he kicked it in, the sound of splintering wood echoing through the quiet.

Keno, with his gun drawn, swept through the top three levels in record time. He moved quickly because he knew the basement level was where his girl was. With the upper levels secured, he cautiously opened the basement door.

Come on, Temu, he thought as he stepped into the darkness. *Don't fail me now.*

Chapter Forty

"Let's see, we've packed all the decorations, all our books and office stuff, and the kitchen is packed up. Let's get started packing up your bedroom, Tucker. Since you told Coach you weren't going to be at today's practice, we have time to tackle that job. What do you say?" Shelly asked as they sat watching Max barking at a squirrel up in a tree. "Tim and Nikki are going to come help us take a load of boxes over tonight."

Tucker shook his head as he took a long drink of sweet tea. "I can do my room myself, Mama Shelly. Ya don't need to help. Ya got enough to do."

"Nah, it's what us moms do. Come on. No time like the present, right? Isn't that what they say? Let's go get started," Shelly said, entering his bedroom. "You know, you've grown so much that I do believe that we can pass along a lot of your clothes to the clothing closet at church instead of packing them. Let's start a separate pile for them."

The longer they worked packing in Tucker's room, the more Shelly noticed him becoming increasingly quiet and tense. *Lord, what is going on? Teenagers are such a mystery to me, but there just seems to be something even stranger going on here. I could sure use your wisdom and guidance here.* The packing kept getting interrupted with Max coming in with his ball and demanding that one of them throw it for him.

When Shelly stepped over to Tucker's closet and opened the door to start working there, Tucker rushed over, nearly tripping over Max. "Why don't I pack this up since I'm taller?" he blurted out.

"Son, what in blazes is going on with you? Are you hiding a girl in here or something?" she demanded with her hands on her hips. Getting no response, she continued standing there waiting for an answer that never came.

Tucker's face flushed, but he stayed quiet. Shelly crossed her arms. "Spill it, Tuck, either tell me or I will tear this closet apart until I find whatever it is that has you so out of sorts."

Tucker fidgeted, swallowing hard before blurting out, "It's jest that…it's…um…It's not mine! I swear!" His voice cracking on the last word.

"Tuck! Start talking or I'm calling Curly to come home and help me pack." Shelly's voice softened. "Now you know you can tell me anything. Anything! And I will love you no matter what! Now, again—what is going on?"

Tucker threw himself on his bed, rolling away from her and mumbled, "It's in the Nike shoebox in the back of the shelf behind my stack of Xbox games. But I promise that it's not mine! A friend just keeps it here!"

Shelly's heart raced. *What on earth?* With a deep breath, she moved the games aside and pulled the shoebox off the shelf. For a fleeting moment, she braced herself for something like a snake or a mouse. Then, with trembling hands, she lifted the lid, and her stomach sank.

"Oh, Tuck," she whispered. "Son, no!"

* * *

Curly, Willis, and Alan watched from the hilltop as the SWAT team converged upon Alan's house. The radio crackled with updates, and when word came that the back door had been kicked open, they were all confident that they would have the man in custody within minutes.

Willis followed the team's movements through his earpiece, giving updates in real time. "They're clearing the rooms now," he said, eyes focused. "Okay, they're approaching the basement and heading toward the safe room now. Shouldn't be much longer."

The tension was thick, but just moments later, Willis's expression twisted to confusion. "What!? How can that be? I'll tell him." He turned to Al. "You can disarm the safe room. There's no one else in the house."

Curly's jaw dropped. "What? The back door was kicked in! We need to spread out and start searching these woods immediately! He has to be close by!" His eyes darted wildly, desperately scanning the tree line for any movement and to hopefully catch a glimpse of the man running through the trees.

Willis let out a long sigh. "Give it up, man. He's long gone by now. My men can see where he tried to breach the safe room, and when he failed, he must've realized he didn't have much time, so he left. He knew there were police everywhere."

"I still think we should at least look around here for him. What do you think, Al?"

"Here comes Tolley, Kimmy, and Daisy. Daisy has a great nose and is trained to search around the perimeter of my house. I'll have her run around and search. She'll let us know if anyone is out there, but I agree with Willis. The guy is a pro, so he's long gone by now."

"Well, since our department doesn't have a search dog, I'll gladly accept Daisy's services. I'll alert my guys as well to keep an eye out." After Curly got off the phone with his dispatcher, Sheila, he turned with a huge smile on his face to the men and said, "Finally, some good news! A North Carolina trooper spotted a dirty white van with a broken taillight headed east, so he hung back and followed it. Right now, this van is parked out at a farmhouse on the outskirts of Raleigh. Didn't Kimmy say that they would have houses along the way for the girls to use the restroom and get water and food? This could be our guy. Let's get Kimmy back to the station and to her parents. Then we'll sit down and draw up a plan to rescue these other girls."

Alan raised his hand, "Hold up just a minute there, Curly, I have a suggestion. This here is a small town where news travels faster than grass through a goose as my granny would say. And this operation has been set up here for a while now, so we don't know who all is part of their network. Be very careful who knows about the trooper spotting this van. I would suggest keeping it off the radios."

Curly sighed in frustration as he looked off into the distance for a minute or two. "As much as I hate to admit it, you are right. No one can keep anything quiet around here." Just then Curly's phone rang. "Hold on, my wife is calling. Hey, honey, what's up? What? Say that again. I couldn't have heard you right." After listening to what Shelly had discovered in Tucker's closet, Curly disconnected the phone and stood there in shock.

Seeing his pale face, Willis, Tolley, and Alan exchanged uneasy glances. Finally, Alan broke the silence. "Hey, man, you okay? Is your wife and kid okay?"

Curly blinked as if snapping out of a daze. "Huh? Oh yeah, yeah. They're fine. Hey, I need to go take care of something. Willis, can you and Tolley make sure Kimmy gets to her parents safely? I'll meet ya'll at the station in a couple of hours."

Without waiting for a reply, Curly turned and went back to his vehicle, which was still parked back at Hillview Drive at the barn. With each step, he prayed for wisdom and guidance.

Chapter Forty-one

Keno had Marshall send a car to pick him up a mile down the road from Alan's property. Completely frustrated with the failed attempt at breaching the safe room, he started reaching out to his network, determined to see if anyone had any information on where they were taking Kimmy next.

Within minutes, he received word that she was being transported to the police station, where she would meet her parents, who were flying in from Florida. The biggest problem was that she was constantly surrounded by police officers and agents.

That idiot Murray! Keno snarled under his breath. *This whole fiasco is his fault! Now I have to figure out a way to get to her from inside a police station!*

Gritting his teeth, he called his source at the station. "You know who this is. Remember, we know where your elderly father lives, and if you don't continue with our little agreement, we won't hesitate to kill him. I also expect you to find a way to get me inside the police station *tonight*." Disconnecting the call, he couldn't help smiling, knowing the distress he had caused to the person on the other end of the call.

Just seconds later, his phone dinged with an incoming text:

"NC trooper is watching a white van at a house outside Raleigh. Will leave back door

to station unlocked after 6 pm. Best I can do.
Now leave me alone."

I KNEW Murray wouldn't spot a tail! What an imbecile! Now I have to solve THAT problem!

Meanwhile, back at the station, the agents tried to make Kimmy as comfortable as possible. Seeing how scared she was, Sheila bustled into the room carrying a bag of chips and a can of Dr. Pepper.

"Yer parents called a little while ago," Shiela said softly. "They're in the air right now and should be landing in about thirty minutes. The Greensboro police will bring them straight over, so they should be here within an hour or so." She set the snacks in front of the girl. "Are ya hungry? You name it, and we have it. Pizza, hamburger, chicken sandwich, whatever ya want we will get for ya. Bless yer heart, honey, after what you've been through, you deserve whatever ya want." Sheila offered, trying to make Kimmy as comfortable as possible.

Kimmy gave her a small smile. "A burger and fries would be wonderful. Thank you so much! You're so kind."

"Well, land's sakes, girl. It's the least we can do. I jest pray we can get the rest of them girls." Sheila waddled off to have one of the deputies make a run to the Dogs-n-Taters to get the order for Kimmy.

* * *

"Let me see it, Shelly." Looking into the shoebox, Curly's stomach dropped as he stared at its contents. There was no longer any use denying that Shelly had been correct in what she had said on the phone. He lowered his voice, filled with disbelief. "What is he thinking?"

"He claims they're not his. That's all he has said."

Curly exhaled deeply and nodded. "Let's go talk to him."

They entered Tucker's room to find him in the same position, still on the bed facing the wall. "Son, sit up and face me, please. We need to have a face-to-face talk."

Tucker slowly rolled over and sat up with his back against the headboard. He kept his head down, his eyes fixed on his lap, avoiding his parents' gaze.

"Please put your head up and look at us," Curly pressed gently. "I want to know why you have a rock of heroin and all this drug paraphernalia hidden in here." Curly patted Tucker's knee but kept a stern look on his face as he continued, "And I want the whole truth. I can handle anything as long as it's the truth. Look at me, please."

"I promise; it's not mine. It's a friend's." Tucker's voice trembled as he looked at Curly through his hair hanging over his eyes.

"So you've said already. Why on earth would you let a friend keep this here? And why would you be friends with someone who is doing any drugs, let alone heroin?"

Tucker hesitated, his eyes darting toward the floor. "He just handed me the box and asked me to put it in my closet because his parents were always snooping in his room. I didn't even look in it until I got home! Then, when I asked him about it, he said that he only does it every once in a while and that he's not an addict or anything.

Curly sighed deeply, running a hand down his face. "That's what they all say. Again, who is this friend? I need a name."

"I don't want to get him in trouble."

Curly's tone sharpened. "Tuck, let me explain something to you. I'm a police officer. Do you even know how much trouble *I* could get into for having any kind of drugs on my property, whether I knew about them or not? Also, if you don't tell us who this friend is then we are going to think this stuff is yours. Now, I don't see any track marks on your arms, and I've never seen you nodding off. However, that doesn't mean you haven't tried it."

"No! I promise! I would never!" Tucker shouted as he looked straight into Curly's eyes.

"Then whose drugs are these?" Curly asked, holding up the showbox. "This is very serious. They need help, Tuck."

Tucker kicked his foot against the wall and muttered a name under his breath.

"Well, I have pretty good hearing, but I wasn't able to hear that. Speak up, son. Who?"

The boy swallowed hard. "Darryl White. But don't tell him I said anything!"

"Have I met this Darryl White? I don't recall meeting him."

"No, he's on my football team. You and Mama Shelly wouldn't approve of him, so I haven't brought him home. But he's jest got crappy parents!"

"Thank you for trusting us enough to tell us his name," Curly said. "Tuck, just because someone is on your team doesn't mean you have to be friends with him. You have to carefully choose your friends. A wrong choice in a friend can lead to a lifetime of hurt and misery. I see it all the time, every day at work. Good kids led astray by bad friends."

Curly paused, his gaze softening. "Now, I want you to text this Darryl and invite him over for pizza tonight. I want to meet him and get to know him."

"Curly, are you sure about this?" Shelly asked as she rubbed Max's head.

He gave a firm nod. "Well, he's already friends with him. Seems like we should get to know him too." Turning back to Tucker, Curly said, "Now get up, Tuck, and help your mama pack up this closet while I head back into work. And, Tuck?"

"Yes, sir?" Tucker replied hesitantly.

"I love you, son, and always will, no matter what," Curly said as he ruffled his hair.

Tuck let out a huge sigh and grinned. "Love you too, Dad."

Chapter Forty-two

It took some maneuvering, but Keno was finally able to locate another passenger van and drivers to pick up the girls from the house outside of Raleigh. Now, it was time to deal with Murray.

When the call connected, Keno didn't wait for pleasantries. "Listen, you idiot," he snapped. "You've been followed just as I expected. A North Carolina trooper followed you and is watching the house right now. So, here's what's going to happen. I've got another van on the way, and it will be there in an hour. They're going to come in the back way, so the trooper won't see them. They'll park in the shed.

"Once they arrive, you are to take the white van and get back on Interstate 40, but instead of heading to Wilmington, I want you to go to Jacksonville, North Carolina. Got it? Once there, find a cheap hotel and stay put until you hear from me. Do. You. Understand? Try not to screw this up any further!"

Before Murray could respond, Keno disconnected and began making plans for getting to Kimmy in the police station.

* * *

The police station was a madhouse when Curly returned. He was relieved to see Kimmy busy eating and chatting with two older folks who he assumed were her parents. Taking a quick detour by that room, he popped his head in and introduced himself. "Hello, I'm Lieutenant Rogers. Anything I can get for any of ya'll?"

The woman stood up, her face lighting up with gratitude. "Oh, Lieutenant! We're Mr. and Mrs. Thornberry, Kimmy's mom and dad—Sheri and Chip. Thank you so very much for getting our little girl back for us! We can't ever thank you enough!" Sheri gushed as tears ran down her face, and Chip stood awkwardly with his hands in his pockets.

"Well, the credit really belongs to this fine young lady," he said, gesturing toward Kimmy. "Her quick thinking and spunk saved her from being sold into slavery. We're just trying to keep her safe while we tie all the loose ends up and find the men who took her."

"Um, these agents were just saying we can't take her back to Fort Lauderdale tonight? We'd really like to just take her home," Chip said.

"Yes, sir, I understand; and we're sorry, but it's for her safety," Curly said. "It seems this trafficking ring goes from Fort Lauderdale all the way up here and probably to the coast of North Carolina. So until we get the people behind the operation, Kimmy will be safest with us. However, I know a police station isn't very comfortable. Give me and these agents some time to talk things over, and we'll see what we can work out, okay?"

At the Thornberry's hesitant nods, Curly smiled and then motioned for Willis and Tolley to follow him to the conference room down the hall.

"Everything okay at home, Curly?" Willis asked as Curly shut the door.

"Yeah, we're good. Go ahead and take a seat. Willis, what's

our plan for Kimmy, and what's the plan for the van and house in Raleigh?" Curly asked as everyone got settled.

Curly took his place at the head of the table and looked at the two agents. "In a perfect world, I would like to keep Kimmy locked up here in the police station, but I highly doubt her parents would agree to that. Am thinking I need to have the field office send a couple of female agents and put them all up at a hotel in Winston-Salem. That way, we can still have eyes on her while giving her parents some peace of mind."

Tolley frowned. "That's an interesting idea, but if the agents are coming from Charlotte, it could take a couple of hours, and we might not have them in place until tomorrow morning."

Curly leaned back in his chair, stretching out his long legs. "I was mulling this over on my way back. We need to do something to draw this guy out. Since this station leaks worse than a rusty faucet, everyone and their cousin now knows that Kimmy is here at the station, and that gives us the perfect opportunity.

"Let's have her parents leave out the front and go check in at that bed and breakfast just down the street. Then I get one of our female deputies, I know just the one, to put on Kimmy's clothes and a wig to match. We put a cot in here for 'Kimmy' to sleep on and leave it unlocked since she's a witness."

Curly leaned forward, resting his elbows on the table. "We then sneak the real Kimmy out the back door into the back of my car. I'll take her to my new place which is out in the middle of a huge farm. And we don't tell anyone about this. Just us three, the deputy, and Kimmy will know.

"You two will take up watch in the next room to see if this guy shows up. If he doesn't show? Great! If he does? Even better. What do you think?"

Willis and Tolley looked at each other for a couple of minutes. Willis tapped his pen on the table while he thought about it; then he shrugged and nodded in agreement, "Works for me, as long as you can keep a very tight lid on who knows about it."

"True," Curly nodded. "But it would be our best chance to catch the guy."

"Alright," Willis said. "Let's do it. But no mistakes, Curly. This has to go off without a hitch." Tolley and Curly nodded.

"Now about the van and house in Raleigh," he continued. "I've already been in contact with the field office there. They've put a team together and are getting ready as we speak. Hold on a minute. They're calling now."

Curly and Tolley waited impatiently as Willis nodded and kept saying repeatedly, "Yes, sir" and "I understand."

When he finally ended the call, Curly said, "What was that about?"

"I think we have a leak," he said cautiously, "and I think it's somewhere in your department."

"MY department?" Curly shot to his feet. "I don't think so! No way!" Curly leaned over the table and got in Willis' face. "What makes you say that?"

Willis held up a hand. "Simmer down and back off, Curly. Let me explain. After sitting there for most of the afternoon, the trooper saw the van finally leave the house. This was about thirty minutes before our team was going to raid it. He was ordered to pull the van over in a routine traffic stop, which he proceeded to do. He had the man, a Murray Williams, get out of the van, but there wasn't anyone else inside."

"Empty?" Tolley asked.

"Completely," Willis confirmed. "But the trooper reported that the van reeked of human excrement. There are outstanding bench warrants on Mr. Williams, so he's in our custody, but, of course, he has lawyered up."

"That still doesn't explain you saying I have a leak," Curly said, crossing his arms.

Willis's eyes narrowed. "Think about it, Curly. How did they know the raid was coming? When our team raided the house, it was empty, but it was obvious that there had been girls held there. Food wrappers and water bottles were strewn everywhere. And the timing of the whole thing. They stayed there all afternoon, and just thirty minutes before we showed up, they were gone? Nah, I'm not buying it. Someone leaked it."

Curly shook his head while rubbing both hands through his curly hair. "But who? We were the only ones who knew!"

"Oh, come on, man! Your dispatcher called and told you. She was probably sitting at her desk out there, which means that at least half the department overheard her telling you," Willis admonished him. "Literally, it could be anyone in this department."

Curly groaned and began pacing again. "Don't tell me I have a trafficker on my staff! These people are my friends! They're my family!"

Willis held his hand up and tried to calm the lieutenant down. "Don't go leaping to conclusions until we know what's going on here. With these rings, we've seen all sorts of things. They'll extort or threaten their own grandmother to get information from someone. So, it could be someone who's been backed into a very uncomfortable corner. Honestly, the more I think about it, the more I like your plan for the Kimmy double. Just don't tell anyone."

"Okay! Okay!" *Lord, what a mess! Please help this plan tonight to work and on top of all this, I'm really worried about Tuck. Please give me wisdom and direction to guide him and keep him safe!*

Chapter Forty-three

Curly left Willis and Tolley in the conference room while he went to his office. After shutting his door, he called Sheila over the intercom, "Hey, I'm way behind on a bunch of my paperwork. I'm not to be interrupted for the rest of the day unless someone dies. Got it?" *That should give me some privacy.*

He then sent a text to Deputy Crissy Martin, a young twenty-two-year-old who was responsible for visiting the schools and teaching the kids about the dangers of drugs.

"Deputy, this is Lieutenant Rogers. I know this is very unusual for me to text you; however I have a very important and highly confidential job for you. Do you know Shelly's friend, Nicole? Do you know Nicole's dad's farm?"

"Yes, sir, to both."

"Meet me there in 30 minutes, and this is highly confidential. DO NOT tell anyone. I'll explain when I see you."

Next, he sent a text to Shelly.

"Take Tucker and go to Nicole's dad's farm, but stay in the house. I'm meeting someone there, and it's confidential. Will explain tonight."

"Of course. We'll take some boxes over with
us. Love you."

"Love you more."

Curly sighed and leaned back in his office chair. *Lord, please
give me wisdom. Help this to work tonight. It sure would be nice for
this to all be wrapped up tonight. And I really don't like keeping secrets
from Shelly and my team.* After talking things over with the Lord,
he felt much calmer, and he had an idea.

Picking up his phone again, he sent out another text, this time
to his brother:

"Chad, meet me in 30 minutes at Nicole's
dad's farm. Keep your lips zipped about this.
TELL NO ONE! I mean it."

Feeling better, he left his office and headed out to meet Deputy
Martin and Chad. As he reached the front of the station, Sheila
called out, "That don't look like no paperwork that I ever saw, and
I ain't heard tell of anyone dying in the last five minutes."

Curly waved her off and said, "I'll be back in an hour. Shelly
needs my help with some boxes. Tell Willis and Tolley to keep a
close eye on Kimmy."

Jogging down the steps, he ducked around the corner to avoid
getting stopped by Jed, who was ambling down the sidewalk.
Twenty minutes later, as he pulled into the driveway that would be
his new home, a small smile tugged at his lips. All the open space
was exactly what the family needed.

Deputy Martin hadn't arrived yet, but Chad was already there, leaning casually against the front of his truck.

"Hey, bro! You call! I come running!" Chuckling, he straightened up and then grew serious when he noticed the expression on Curly's face. "Seriously, what's going on that you needed me here and on the down low?"

Curly didn't mince words. "Did you tell anyone, and I mean anyone that I asked to meet you here?"

"No! You said zipped lips!" Chad huffed, all offended.

"Knock off the attitude," Curly snapped. "This is a life and death situation, and I gotta be sure that you didn't leak it. Did you tell that new girlfriend of yours where you're going? What's her name? Joelle? Does she know?"

Chad put his hands up. "I promise ya, no one, not even Joelle knows that I am here. Joelle's still at work. Dude, what are you so worked up about? And who is that pulling into your driveway if this is so secret?"

"That's Deputy Crissy Martin. I'll explain to both of you at the same time. I asked you to be here because, other than Shelly, you are the only person in this town that I can completely trust. And tonight I need someone that I can completely trust to help me with a little something that we have going on."

After Crissy exited her vehicle and joined the men standing by Chad's truck, Curly explained the plan, describing how she would act as Kimmy's double that night at the station. The plan was when the shift change approached, Chad would have Crissy put on a wig and lie down in the back of his cruiser with a black blanket over her.

"Excuse me, Lieutenant." Deputy Martin interrupted, "Where's this wig?"

"Oh, good question. I believe we have one from the church's fall festival costume party. It's either here or at my apartment. I'll get it here to you in time."

"Once at the station, Chad will text me that you've arrived, and I'll call for a meeting out front with all the officers so that you can sneak into the cell where we have Kimmy. Once there, you two switch clothes and the real Kimmy leaves with Chad. Chad, you'll then bring Kimmy here and hide her in the house."

Chad stood there with his mouth open, then cleared his throat. "Um, wow! From knocking on doors to this! Awesome!"

Curly shook his head, glancing at his watch. "As long as you take it seriously," he said. "I've been gone too long. Remember, no one, and I mean *no one*, is to know about this. Not even Shelly. Deputy, we'll make sure you're safe. Agents Willis and Tolley will be guarding you at the station. Now, any questions before I go find a wig?"

They took a few minutes to iron out all the details and clear up any confusion before Curly handed them water bottles and a bag of snacks. "Stay here in the car until it's time. I'll be back shortly with that wig."

He called Shelly as he walked to his car. "Hey, did you see that blonde wig while packing?"

"Actually, I just packed it this morning," she replied. "It's in one of the boxes we brought to the new place."

"Great, I'm actually walking in now and will get it from you."

***

When Curly walked into the farmhouse, Shelly put her hand on her hip and raised her eyebrows. "So, I'm a bit curious as to why my big handsome husband needs a woman's long, blonde wig in the middle of a big case. But this is me *not* asking," Shelly teased as she handed it to him with a quick kiss.

"Thanks, honey. I promise I'll explain soon. See you for supper." Curly gave her a wink and hurried off.

After passing the wig to Deputy Martin, Curly rushed back to the station. As he entered, Sheila called out, "Jed stopped by but left after he had waited half an hour. Did you get the missus all taken care of? I told ya you shoulda gotten a moving company or gotten our guys to move ya." She popped her gum as she sat at the front desk.

"Oh, we're fine. We're almost done. Tim and Nikki are getting some of the teens from church to come help tomorrow. By the way, send out a notice to everyone on shift that I want to hold a meeting out front at shift change. I need to update everyone." Curly smacked the countertop. "Okay, I'm going back to my office and the mountain of paperwork." And he strolled down the hallway to check on Kimmy.

Curly shut the door and told the agents that all was ready for that night and that his brother was doing the driving. Both agents erupted out of their seats at the news that he had included someone new in the operation without their approval.

"You're *brother*? What part of tell no one didn't you understand?" Willis shouted as he pointed his finger at Curly.

"You can yell all you want. It's done. And I needed someone to drive the girls back and forth while I keep my officers busy. And there's no one that I trust more in this world than Chad. He WILL keep his lips sealed."

"Well, he better or your head will roll," Willis growled.

Chapter Forty-four

Keno spent the afternoon confirming with his sources that Kimmy was still inside the police station. He then got back on the phone with Temu, his tech guy. "Hey, man, any chance that you could tap into the cameras of the Pilotview Police Station? I don't need them disabled; I just need eyes inside."

Temu laughed. "That's a cakewalk for me, dude. Way easier than that safe room. If I had just had five minutes more, I could have gotten you in there."

"Temu, my man, no worries! Hey, you saved my butt. If you hadn't been watching the cameras and seen that a SWAT team was approaching, I'd be in the slammer now. So just chill. We're all good. Our merchandise is in this police station, and I have a way in after six p.m. tonight. I just want you to get eyes inside to guide me. Can you do it?"

"Man, you're giving me three hours warning? Of course I can do it! A baby could do it! In fact, I'll go ahead and start monitoring the cameras now. You text me when you're ready to enter, and I'll guide you straight to her."

"Thanks, man. I'll settle up with you when I get back to Fort Lauderdale."

Keno checked in with the van drivers and was relieved to find out that they had reached the holding place in Wilmington and had the girls secured there.

He glanced at the clock. *Okay, I have twenty-four hours before the boss shows up to get Kimmy to Wilmington. And after tonight? Murray will be history after Chico sticks a shiv in him. That's what he gets for messing this whole thing up. Now, that door better be unlocked tonight…*

* * *

Curly was actually making progress on his reports when Tolley walked in and closed the door behind him. "I'd offer you a chair, but as you can see, it's pretty cramped in here," Curly said as he looked around at the stacks of files and papers piled up on every available surface.

Tolley leaned against the wall and said, "This will be short anyways. Willis and I were just reviewing everything for tonight. Great plan by the way. But something occurred to me, and Willis agreed."

"What's that?" Curly asked as he leaned back in his chair and stretched.

"This human trafficking ring is well organized and connected. Out at Al's place, they somehow managed to take down his cameras and security system. And this station? It's got cameras everywhere."

"Hold that thought." Curly tapped a couple of keys on his keyboard. "Go on. I just disabled the camera in here."

Tolley nodded approvingly. "You're on the same page as we are. They could be watching us even now, which is no big deal, but it will be a huge deal when we do the switch with Kimmy. So Willis and I have a thought."

Curly interrupted, "We'll just turn the cameras off."

"No, no. That won't work. That would be way too obvious. This guy would smell a trap a mile away if we did that. Here's the plan: when Chad gets to the parking lot, and you're out front with everyone, I'll pretend to slip into the bathroom. Except I'll step into the server room and unplug the system. I'll text Chad. Let the girls switch out, and once Deputy Martin is in place, I'll plug it back up."

Curly started nodding. "Yeah, I like it. Our system glitches all the time, so everyone will believe it. In fact, why don't we do it now for five minutes? That way, the leak can assure them that it's just a glitch."

Tolley stood straight up and pointed at Curly. "Now you're thinking! I'll go do it now!"

A few minutes later, there was a knock at Curly's door and Sheila popped her head around the door. "No one's dead, sir, but is your computer working? Mine just went out again. Stupid thing goes in and out all the time."

"Believe it or not, I've not been on the computer all afternoon. Let me check." Curly swiveled around and attempted to power his computer on. When nothing happened, he shrugged and said, "It's down too. Looks like we've had another glitch. Give it a couple of minutes and try again. We really need city council to do an upgrade on our system."

Sheila hmphed, shaking her head. "Like they'll spend a red cent on anything for us. Alrighty, I'll leave you alone so you can get back to your paperwork." She left and shut the door behind her.

Five minutes later, she called over the intercom, "Boss, we're back online. Another strange glitch indeed."

"Good. Thanks for the update." Curly sent Tolley a text:

"Dispatcher is convinced it's a glitch, so the whole town will soon know about it."

Tolley sent back a thumbs up along with:

"Let me know when Chad arrives."

* * *

Crissy and Chad had spent a boring couple of hours waiting, but it was finally time to head into town. Crissy donned her wig and took her position in the back seat with the blanket over her. Chad texted Curly his ETA and kept reminding himself to breathe normally. *You have nothing to be nervous about! You're just the driver!*

As he sat at a red light, waiting for it to change to green, he received a text from Joelle:

"Hey, sugar, dinner at my place?"

Oh no! he thought. *What am I gonna say to her that isn't a lie?*

He thought long and hard about it, and at the next red light he sent her a reply:

"Sorry, babe, Curly needs my help with the move. I'll text you in a bit. Driving."

When he got to the light right before the police station, he texted Curly:

"Pulling in now."

Curly's response was immediate:

"Have Deputy Martin wait in car ten minutes."

Chad pulled into a shaded spot under a tree and turned to Crissy. "Stay put. We have orders to wait for ten minutes."

Inside the station, Curly texted Tolley to turn off the cameras and then went out front to meet with his officers. Sheila had done her job well. The only ones in the back of the station were the agents and Kimmy; everyone else was waiting for him in the front meeting room.

When he entered, they all came to attention. "At ease, everyone. We have a lot to cover." For the next half hour, Curly updated his officers on all that had transpired, starting with the mall bombing and ending with Kimmy's being in protective custody.

Meanwhile, Kimmy and Crissy quickly changed outfits and places. Deputy Martin seamlessly took Kimmy's place on the cot while Chad led Kimmy out to his car and had her lie down under the blanket. "It's not far; I promise."

That went easier than expected. Thank you, Lord.

"In conclusion, the FBI is actively pursuing the human trafficking ring that kidnapped Kimmy. If you see anything suspicious or anyone acting suspiciously, please do not try to handle it on your own. You are to report it directly to me. Dismissed." After chatting with several of his officers, Curly returned to the conference room.

"Boss, hold up," Sheila called out.

"Yes, Sheila?"

"The system glitched again while ya were in yer meeting. This is getting to be ridiculous. How's a person supposed to get anything done around here with a computer popping on and off?" she demanded as she smacked her gum.

"Again? Yeah, will definitely report it to the council. Let me check on our girl before I head home for dinner. Have a good one, Sheila." Curly opened the door to the conference room and asked, "Anyone need anything in here before I head home?"

Both agents shook their heads as Willis said, "Sheila's bringing us something from the Dog-n-Taters. I just checked on Kimmy. She's napping."

"Okay. See ya'll in the morning. Call me if you need anything." *Okay, Lord, please protect Deputy Martin and please let this plan work.*

Chapter Forty-five

Since Chad had brought Kimmy to the farm, Shelly had been busy in the kitchen, baking homemade pizzas for everyone. Darryl's parents had dropped him off earlier in the afternoon, and now he and Tucker were out front throwing the football around, while Max chased the ball, barking happily.

When Curly pulled into the drive and saw the boys playing, he suddenly remembered. *Oh, man! I completely forgot Darryl was coming over tonight! Probably not the best idea with Kimmy here, but too late now.*

Parking the car, he walked over to the boys and introduced himself to Darryl with a firm handshake. Then he threw the ball around with them for a few minutes before heading inside to find Shelly standing at the kitchen sink, gazing out the window with a huge smile on her face.

"Now that's a fantastic sight to come home to! My gorgeous wife smiling and happy. What has put such a beautiful smile on your face tonight?" he asked as he pulled her in for a hug and a kiss.

"Just seeing Tuck and Max outside having so much space to run around! I swear Max is grinning as much as Tuck is!" Turning around from the window, she spread out her arms, "And look at how much room I have in this kitchen! What a blessing!"

Her tone shifted as she tilted her head toward the family room.

"Now, are you going to tell me why your brother and a stranger are sitting in the family room? Thank goodness Nikki left some furniture behind. And what on earth did you need a wig for?" She swatted him playfully with her dish towel, then put her hands on her hips.

"The boys are still outside, right?" At Shelly's nod, Curly explained what all had been going on that day. "Now I wasn't supposed to tell you all that, so keep it to yourself. It seems we have a leak in my department, as much as it hurts me to say that."

Her mouth dropped open. "Curly! Surely not! I can't think of a single person who'd betray you like that! And especially with human traffickers!" Shelly said as she turned to start putting toppings on her pizzas.

Curly shook his head and rubbed the back of his neck. "It has me completely baffled. And it's killing me to not trust my officers. But as of right now, it's a very small group who know what I just told you about. Let's eat and get Darryl on his way. With Kimmy staying here, I'm not really comfortable with having him here too long. Let me check on her and Chad while you finish up the pizzas."

In the family room, Kimmy was stretched out on the couch watching television while Chad sat in the recliner, playing games on his phone.

"Hey, Kimmy, you hanging in there okay? Hopefully, this ends tonight," Curly said.

"I'm good. Just ready to get back home. I do appreciate you all putting me up, though."

"No problem at all." He then turned to his brother. "Chad, everything go okay with the switch? Any problems?"

"Nah, no problems," he replied casually, then he hesitated. "Joelle texted while we were on our way—"

Curly interrupted before he could finish, "What? You didn't say—"

"Chill, dude. Of course not! I told her you needed my help with moving. So put me to work unpacking boxes so it's not a lie, please."

Curly showed him where Shelly had stacked several boxes to be unpacked and put him to work. While Chad was busy doing that, Curly went to help Shelly finish up dinner. As they worked in the kitchen, they chatted about who they thought the leak could or could not be, never realizing that the boys had come inside and were standing in the mudroom listening to every word.

Dinner was very relaxed with everyone asking Kimmy about life in Florida. The boys got really excited when she told them that they had alligators living everywhere around them. When she told Tucker that she had actually seen an alligator eat a turtle in a pond in her community, he peppered her nonstop with questions about any other wildlife she had seen.

Laughing, Curly finally interrupted, "Knock it off, Tuck. She's not an alligator expert. Let her eat her pizza."

"Oh, sorry, Kimmy."

Kimmy grinned and said, "It's okay; you remind me of my little brother. I really miss him."

When they were all stuffed from Shelly's amazing pizza, Curly told her to leave the dishes for later and to come with him and the boys to the back porch. "Bring your tea with you, fellas. Chad, you and Kimmy make yourselves comfortable in the family room. We'll be back in a few minutes."

Once they were all seated on the porch, Curly looked at Darryl. "Has Tucker told you why we invited you over tonight?"

Darryl nervously looked at Tucker as he replied, "He jest said ya'll wanted to meet me."

Curly sat back in the rocking chair and stretched out his legs to get comfortable as he nodded. "That's true. We did want to meet you. However, as you can see, we're in the process of moving, and as we were packing up Tucker's closet, we came across a Nike shoebox. Do you want me to say what I found in that box?"

Darryl's face turned pale, and he dropped his head.

"Darryl?" Curly leaned forward to see Darryl's face better. "Do *you* know what was in this box?"

Darryl kept his head down as he nervously nodded.

"Now, I noticed earlier that you have a couple of marks on your arms where you have probably already played around with heroin."

When Darryl started shaking his head, Curly held his finger up. "Look at me now." When Darryl met his eyes, Curly continued, "Son, I'm a police officer. I'm not a fool. Don't ever even think of lying to me. Is that your shoebox that I found?"

Darryl dropped his head again and just sat there with his hair hanging in his face.

"I need an answer unless you want me to call your parents."

At that, Darryl looked up and replied, "Please don't call them. It's my box."

"Thank you. Now, where did you get those items?"

Darryl's head shot up in panic. "Please! I can't tell you that! I can't! He'll kill me!"

"Okay," Curly nodded slowly. "We'll come back to that later. This is how this is gonna go. I could arrest both of you boys for possession, which is a felony." At that, Shelly gasped, and Curly reached over and put his hand over hers. "Consider this your one-time free pass. Darryl, you are now on my radar, which means you are now on the radar of every officer who works in Pilotview. If you so much as THINK of doing something wrong, you will be in juvie so quick you won't know what happened. You understand?"

When Darryl nodded furiously, Curly leaned forward and continued, "Good. Now, you seem like a decent kid who has just maybe made a couple of bad decisions. I'm going to talk to your parents about getting you to help out with some chores around Central Park for money after school and on the weekend. Also, if you and Tuck are gonna remain friends, then I expect to see you in church. You okay with all of that?"

"Yes, sir! Thank you! I'm awfully sorry for giving that box to Tucker. I know that was dumb. Sorry, Tuck."

"It's okay," Tucker replied.

"And, Tuck, remember—this is your one free pass as well. Next time, you come to me or your mama first. We can help. Otherwise, you face the consequences, understand?"

"Yes, sir," Tucker replied quickly.

"Um, sir?" Darryl asked.

"Yes?"

Darryl fidgeted, glancing at Tucker before looking back at Curly. "Tuck and me heard you and Mrs. Rogers talking about how someone in the police station has been telling the kidnappers stuff. I think I might have heard something that might help."

Chapter Forty-six

Curly struggled not to get angry as he drove down old Highway 52 toward Chestnut Grove Road. After Darryl's revelation about what he had overheard while riding in his older brother's car, Curly had been left stunned. At first, he just sat there, staring at the boy in disbelief. Finally, he shook his head as if to clear it, turned toward Shelly and asked, "Surely I just heard him wrong?"

As shocked as he was, she replied with a shaky voice, "If so, I heard the same thing."

So now, he was on his way to confront the one person in the department he never thought would betray him.

Shelly had wanted to come along, hoping to help keep his anger in check, but he knew he needed to keep this official. The sense of betrayal tore at him, and he realized that he needed to start praying because there was no way that he could handle this meeting in his own strength.

Reluctantly, he turned into the driveway and parked next to the house. Instead of getting out, he texted Willis to check on their status to delay the inevitable. He played on his phone for so long that the porch light came on, then the front door opened, and out she stepped.

"Curly? What's wrong? Why are ya jest sittin' there in yer car? Land's sakes! Come on inside! Hush, Boo-Boo," she added, shushing her small dog.

Curly sighed, stepped out of his vehicle, and made his way to the house. When he walked through the door, Boo-Boo, her Maltese dog, greeted him. Then Curly reluctantly said, "Sheila, I…I don't even know where to start. How could you?"

Sheila had been bending over to give Boo-Boo a treat, but at Curly's tone, she looked up, and at the look on his face, she burst out crying. "Oh thank you, Jesus! You know!" she sobbed. "I've been wanting to tell you, but they said they'd kill my daddy! Oh, Curly! It's been killing me knowing I've been helping those wicked, wicked men!" She collapsed onto the couch, crying uncontrollably.

Boo-Boo immediately jumped up and started licking her face and whining. Every time Curly tried to approach to console her, the little dog would turn and growl at him, so he just stepped back and put his hands up.

He sent Shelly a text:

> "You better come on over to Sheila's quick. I
> need help."

While he waited for either Sheila to calm down or Shelly to arrive, he went into the kitchen and made some sweet tea. He also found a package of Oreo cookies and added them to the tray. Just as he was arranging them on the tray, Shelly stepped into the kitchen.

"Boy, am I glad to see you! I can't get her to stop crying! All she has said so far is that they would kill her daddy if she didn't help them, and then she started blubbering. Boo-Boo won't even let me step near her. Do you think you could calm her down?"

"Bless her heart. What did you say to her?"

"Hardly anything! She just looked at me and knew. Please help a guy out here!" Curly pleaded with his wife.

Shelly winked at him as she grabbed an Oreo. "I'll do what I can." It took a bit, but she finally soothed Sheila enough to get her to answer Curly's questions without falling apart.

"Sheila, I can't tell you what a relief it is to know you aren't part of some criminal gang or something. I just could never have believed that! I know how much you love your daddy, though, so tell me, when did this all happen?"

"Oh," she paused as she hiccupped, "a year or so ago."

Curly gasped as he repeated, "A year or so?"

"Yeah, I'm so embarrassed."

Curly shook his head. "No, don't worry about that right now. Just tell me what kinds of information they asked you for."

"Until this week? Nothing really. Just stuff like which officers were working and when did their shifts end and begin. That kind of stuff. But this week they've been calling and texting a lot."

Curly's chest tightened. "Do they know anything about tonight?"

"Tonight? Ohhh…" her face crumpled. "Yeah, Deputy Martin mentioned to me that she was gonna pretend to be Kimmy tonight. And…" Sheila stopped and hung her head.

I swear no one can keep a secret in this town! No one! "Sheila, what? Go on…don't stop now," Curly encouraged, trying not to scare her.

"Well, it's probably too late anyways," she shrugged.

"What does that mean? What do you know?" Curly had to

really work to keep his voice calm as Shelly kept looking over at him with her eyebrows raised.

"He told me if I didn't find a way for him to get into the police station, then my daddy was dead tonight!" she yelled clutching Boo-Boo close to her chest.

"Who is he, and what did you do?" Curly patiently asked again.

"You gotta hurry!" she blurted. "I left the back door of the station unlocked at 6 pm. He could be there now! His name is Keno, but I've never seen him." At that, she fell apart sobbing again as Shelly gathered her into her arms, trying to console her.

Curly's jaw tightened as he pulled out his phone. He realized he still hadn't heard back from Willis. "Shell, can you stay here with Sheila while I go check things out at the station?"

"Of course, but Curly, please take someone with you!" Shelly said.

"I'll send officers to your dad's assisted living and over here, Sheila," Curly reassured her, turning to leave. "But I need to get to the station immediately. Shelly, don't worry. I'll call soon."

He sprinted to his vehicle, making multiple calls to Willis, Tolley, and Deputy Martin but not reaching anyone. He called all of his officers to the station and alerted the FBI field office, explaining the situation and his inability to reach their agents. Their supervisor was already in the process of sending in agents and assured him that help was on the way. The supervisor went on to explain that it would take at least an hour for the assisting agents to arrive from Greensboro.

Curly's grip tightened on the steering wheel as he sped toward the station, praying the agents were just too busy to answer their phones. Deep down, though, he feared that he was going to find something far worse when he arrived.

Chapter Forty-seven

Earlier that evening, after Sheila had left the back door unlocked, Keno waited until dark before slipping into the alley behind the station. Dressed entirely in black, with football grease smeared on his face to blend into the shadows, he crouched behind the dumpsters. After being there a while and observing little activity at the station, he sent a text to check the cameras.

Temu quickly replied:

> "They've had a couple of glitches today, but all appears good. The girl is zonked on a cot in a cell. 2 agents in a room next door with a window to see in. You'll need to take them out."

> "Glitches?"

> "I've checked their history. It's a pretty common thing for them. So no worries. You're good to go."

> "Check. Will have an earbud in. Let me know if trouble comes in. Going soon."

Let's hope Sheila did her job. When he found that the back door was indeed open, he couldn't help but smirk, and then he realized that he could still use her help some more.

He typed out another text:

> "You know who this is. Get those agents
> away from Kimmy in the next hour or you
> know what I will do."

Shelly jumped at Sheila's sudden gasp. "What on earth is that for, Sheila?"

"I thought I was through with him! Here, Shelly, look! It's that evil man again! He just won't leave me alone!" She thrust her phone at Shelly as she collapsed into another fit of sobbing.

Shelly immediately used her phone to call Curly, who called all his officers to re-route to meet him at Sheila's as he did a U-turn. He had an idea of how to use this latest text to their advantage. He turned on his flashers and raced as fast as he could back to her place.

When Curly burst through the door, he found Sheila exactly where he'd left her. Sheila sat clutching Boo-Boo while Shelly held up Sheila's phone and showed him the text.

"This is actually good.," he said, nodding. "We can work with this. The whole department is on their way here. This is what I want you to text as a reply:

> "The lieutenant has everyone out looking for
> you. Agents are hungry, 1 agent leaving to
> get some food in 1 hr."

After she sent the text, Curly's phone rang. He let out a huge whoop when he saw it was from Willis. "Man! You had me worried! Why haven't you answered any of my texts or calls?"

"Sorry, man! We thought we had heard someone sneaking around in here, so we went silent. It turned out to be a false alarm. We are clear now," Willis responded.

"That's a huge relief! Let me tell you what's been going on here! I think we have a chance of getting this guy, finding the van, and hopefully taking down the whole network tonight!" Curly quickly proceeded to fill him in on his plans to trap Keno.

"You know, this could actually work," Willis said. "Okay, in an hour, I'll send Tolley out for some Arby's sandwiches."

"Good. Then Sheila will send him another text that we got an anonymous tip that someone spotted him in Pinnacle. I'll have a couple of my guys run out the front door like they are responding to the lead. She'll tell Keno that's the best time to move in."

"And that's when I'll be inside, ready to nab him," Willis said.

"No," Curly corrected. "Don't forget the cameras. You must continue as usual. My officers and I will come in from behind and take him down. Once we've got him, we'll break him and finally get some answers."

"Well, I've yet to see a plan go the way we want it to, but let's do it!" Willis agreed.

When Keno got Sheila's text that one of the agents would be going out to get dinner in an hour, he nodded and settled in behind the dumpster. He replied,

"Your daddy gets to live another day."

Later, when a second text came through claiming that he'd been spotted in Pinnacle, and he saw officers rushing out of the station, he had to clamp a hand over his mouth to keep from laughing out loud. *Idiots.*

Finally, he saw one of the agents leave to go get their meal, just like his snitch had said he would. *Perfect.* He checked in with Temu once last time.

"All clear," Temu confirmed.

Satisfied, Keno cautiously stood up and approached the back door. Testing the handle, his heart raced as it turned easily. The door creaked as he began to pull it open.

Suddenly, bright lights flashed on and voices erupted from the darkness behind him. "Police! Freeze!"

Chapter Forty-eight

Willis and Tolley stood observing while Curly interrogated Keno. "Let me introduce myself. I'm Lieutenant Greg Rogers; the one in charge here in Pilotview since your crew blew up my mayor and police chief."

Seeing Keno was getting ready to speak, Curly held up his hand. "Hold on; not your turn quite yet. Don't go saying anything yet. I know, I know. You are thinking about asking for a lawyer, but before you do, let me tell you about a really, really sweet deal. It's even in writing, mind ya, for you. And it's direct from the DA. You know, we have you for a whole slew of things."

Curly shuffled some papers around and acted like he was reading as he started his list of offenses. "Let's see . . . Starting with bombings, then conspiracy, kidnapping, human trafficking, and we're just getting started." Curly glanced up and saw Keno wanting to interrupt again, so he pointed his finger and shook his head.

"Nope, I'm still talking here. So, here's this stupidly sweet deal that our DA is making me offer you. If you give us verifiable proof to take down the head of your human trafficking ring *and* you cough up the location of the girls by tomorrow evening? Then, our DA will drop all charges against you. Every last one. I fought the DA long and hard against offering you this deal at all, but he said I *had* to give you fifteen minutes to think it over. It's simple: do you want to be in jail with men who've had sisters abducted by traffickers like you or do you want this ridiculously sweet offer from the DA?" Curly looked at his watch. "Fifteen minutes— starting now."

Keno's jaw tightened. "I want to see it in writing," he said through clenched teeth.

"Of course you do." Curly held his hand up and waved for the DA to enter the room.

The district attorney came in, sat in the chair next to Curly, and pulled the paperwork out of his briefcase. After reviewing it to confirm its accuracy, he handed it over to Keno.

"It is all as the Lieutenant said," the DA confirmed.

Keno read it carefully and signed it with a flourish. After he had signed it, he leaned back in his chair and smirked. "Give me some paper and a pen, and I'll write down the address for those girls. You'd better hurry, though; they're scheduled to be sold at eight a.m."

Curly ripped a piece of paper from his notepad and handed it to Keno along with a pen. He watched as Keno wrote down an address, which appeared to be in the Wilmington area. The moment he finished, Curly snatched the paper and stepped out to confer with the agents.

"We've got the address," Curly yelled to Willis and Tolley. They called the field office to dispatch a SWAT team to rescue the girls.

Knowing the girls would soon be on their way home made Curly feel like he was walking on air. "As soon as you have received word that they are safe, come in and tell me so that we can move on to the next stage," he instructed Willis before heading back into the interrogation room.

Once back inside with Keno, Curly sat down and continued, "Okay, we should hear shortly whether you gave us good information or not. Now, who's the head of this organization? I know it's not the guy we arrested driving the van."

Keno busted out laughing. "Murray? Nah, he's an idiot! He was only responsible for controlling the merchandise in North Carolina and ensuring the girls received food and water."

"Is that why I've had meat being stolen?"

Keno sighed. "I told you—he's an idiot. Yes, he thought if he stole meat from old people that they wouldn't even notice. Like I said: idiot!"

"Did you set the bombs off?" Curly pressed.

"Again, Murray. He thought it would be a good idea to distract you from our operation because we had a shipment coming in. I wasn't even up here when it happened."

"How many in my department are part of your ring?" Curly asked, narrowing his eyes.

"Just Sheila. And she was very reluctant. The only reason she did anything was because we threatened her precious daddy."

"So, if it wasn't you or Murray in charge, then who is it?"

"You don't know her. She lives in Fort Lauderdale. Her name is Anita Batista. All her contact information is on my phone, but good luck. She moves around constantly and blends in like a chameleon. She knows how to disappear so well that a lot of us nicknamed her 'ghost'."

At that moment, Willis stepped into the room, leaned down, and whispered in Curly's ear before leaving. Curly smiled at Keno and said, "Great news! They raided that address and rescued over one hundred and fifty young ladies who were all drugged, waiting to be sold. Your information was credible, so thank you."

At that, Curly stood up and walked to the door. Keno also stood up to leave. Curly turned and asked, "Where do you think you're going?"

"You found the girls, and I gave you Anita's information. I'm out of here. You said no charges, right?"

The door opened, and the two agents stepped inside the room. Tolley smiled coldly. "That's right. *He* did, but we didn't. FBI agents Willis and Tolley. All local charges have been dropped as agreed, but you ARE under arrest for multiple accounts of human trafficking along with…"

As Curly walked down the hallway, he couldn't help but smile at the sound of Keno screaming, "You lied to me!"

Chapter Forty-nine

It had turned out to be a beautiful day for Chad's graduation from the police academy that morning. Curly was now back at the farm relaxing on the front porch watching all their friends and neighbors gathering together to celebrate this milestone in Chad's life. Curly took a moment to reflect on how special it was to hand that badge to his brother as he crossed the stage that morning. After the rough few weeks their town had been through, this day felt extra special. Still, he just wished that their father's health had been good enough to attend or that he was aware enough to fully understand all that his sons had accomplished. *That's okay, at least we have each other.*

"There you are! I've been looking everywhere for you. Are you okay?" Shelly asked as she snuggled onto his lap and played with his hair.

Curly smiled as he answered, "Couldn't be better. Kimmy called earlier after she and her folks landed back in Fort Lauderdale. She'd heard about the other girls being rescued and was just gushing on the phone with gratitude to us and to God that they were all safe. Her parents said that they plan on coming back up here this fall for a family vacation so that they can make some good memories here in good ole' Pilotview." He paused, squinting at the driveway.

"Look there! Is that Ms. Angel and Jed in his old truck? What on earth is Jed doing here? Great! He's going to talk my ear off! Did you have to invite the entire town?"

Shelly laughed and shrugged. "Well, I just think our little ole' town needs a party, and look at all this space that God's blessed us with," she said as she spread her arms wide. She jumped up and pulled him up with her. "Come on, enough reflecting. Let's go find Chad and Joelle. I've been talking to her some today, and I must admit I like her!"

Curly chuckled and followed around to the backyard, where the grill was set up. Max came bounding up, ball in mouth, and Curly threw it as far as he could. Just as the dog tore off after it, he did a double take. "Um, honey? Is that the ER doctor? What's his name?"

"Doctor Catania? Yes, that's him. After all he did for us I wanted him to celebrate with us too. Again, I told you I was inviting everyone that I could think of. Plus, I have a surprise for you and Tuck. Come on!"

"A surprise? I don't think I can take any more surprises, Shell!"

"Oh, hush! It's a good one! A great one, in fact." By this time, they had finally made it to the backyard grill area, where Chad and Tim had taken command of grilling the chicken, burgers, and corn-on-the-cob. Nicole was busy setting out the platters of freshly grilled meat as the men got them grilled. Tucker and his teammates were scattered all around, running plays and tossing the football. Spotting Coach Waddell among the group, Curly went over to encourage him on their tournament the next day.

"So, Coach," he said. "do you know much about one of your players, Darryl?"

Coach shrugged his broad shoulders and sighed. "Have never seen his folks come to practices or a game. I know he's got an older brother who's trouble with a capital 'T'. Why do you ask?" He took a drink of his Coke as he turned and looked at Curly.

Curly grabbed a burger from the platter of meat and took a bite, wiping his mouth. "Wow! That's a great burger! I was just wondering, that's all. Tuck's been hanging out with him some. I'm trying to get to know him better."

Before Curly could ask him anything else, Chad came over and interrupted, "Hey, big brother! Just want to say thanks! Thanks for believing in me and letting me help you some while I was in the academy. Love you, man." At that, he gave him a huge slap on the back.

Curly grinned and said, "Well, I was gonna wait until Monday, but I have some good news. I was just informed by the city council that you've been approved for that position. Come see me Monday morning."

Chad whistled and grinned. "Seriously? Oh man! Yes, thanks! I'll be there! Joelle! Babe! Guess what?" He then ran off to tell her his good news.

Coach and Curly just stood there shaking their heads and laughing. Shelly walked up and kissed him on the cheek. Curly raised his eyebrow. "Not complaining, but what was that for?"

"Your surprise is here. Well, it's really Tuck's surprise. Can you call him in?"

"Hey, Tuck! Come here a sec!" Curly yelled.

Just as Tucker rushed up with the football and Max following closely behind, a dark blue Lexus 330 with West Virginia license plates pulled down the driveway.

"Now, who's here from West Virginia?" Curly asked with raised eyebrows.

"You'll see," Shelly said as she smiled.

After the car stopped, the door opened, and Tucker's grandfather stepped out. "Did I hear there was a party going on? I like a good party!"

"Grandpa? Oh wow!" Tucker dropped the ball and went barreling straight into his grandfather's arms. "Man, it's been ages since I've seen ya."

"Now, son, let a man breathe," his grandfather chuckled, patting him on the back.

Curly pulled Shelly in close and whispered, "Now that's a really nice surprise."

Alan walked up and asked, "Who's the rich guy?"

Curly laughed and replied, "Oh yeah, you're new here. That's Tucker's grandfather. You see, a couple of years back, Tucker was Shelly's sixth-grade student and ended up in a bit of trouble. In fact, it's how she and I met." So he took a few minutes to catch Alan up on all that had happened to Tucker and his family.

Alan whistled. "Tucker's mighty blessed to not only have his grandfather but ya'll. I hate to interrupt, Curly, but can I talk to you for a minute?"

"Of course, what's up?" They walked up to the porch to get some privacy. "What's going on, Al?"

Alan sighed and re-positioned his ballcap. "It looks like I need your help on something."

THE END

Note from Lizzy

I hope you enjoyed going on this adventure with me as much as I have enjoyed writing about Curly, Shelly and Tucker along with the rest of the Pilotview crew. This third book has Tucker struggling with suicidal thoughts along with having a buddy introduce him to the world of drugs. My readers might think that this is going overboard for a boy of this age, so I wanted to share from my heart with you, my awesome readers.

I lost my mother at the age of eleven and struggled horribly with suicidal thoughts for a couple of years before I accepted Jesus as my Savior. (You can read my full testimony on my website, so I won't go through all of it here.) So, I know from my own experience how a child of this age can really struggle with wanting to die. If you know of any child who's lost a parent or gone through any tragedy, please keep talking to them about it. They need adults to understand that it doesn't get better just because it happened a year or so ago. It took years before her death wasn't a constant thought in my life. Also, God sent a very special woman into my life, just when I needed it, who would spend hours just letting me talk. That helped me tremendously.

Then Tucker has a buddy asking him to hide heroin. I can just imagine some of you being shocked that such a thing would happen. I was a middle school teacher for many years, and I'm also a mother of a daughter in recovery from heroin's grasp. (Praise God she's in recovery!) So, I'm very aware that heroin can reach any community, no matter the size, and any child, no matter how well a parent tries to protect them. Drug addiction is awful to not only the person using the drug but also to all who know that person. I tried to keep this part of the book "light," but I also wanted to highlight this problem. More people need to actively look at the children and teens in their lives and pay attention to what they are doing.

Curly, Shelly and Tucker have characteristics similar to people in my life, so I try to have them go through life events that my family and friends have experienced. (Thankfully, we haven't experienced any bombings!) As you know, these three characters pray multiple times a day in quick prayers. This is because I want to give you an example, even fictitiously, of Christians going through difficult times while trusting in God. Life is not always easy, but GOD CAN help us through anything life may throw at us.

If you don't have a relationship with Jesus, I would love to hear from you and chat with you about how Jesus can change your whole life and bring you joy unending. You can email me at shellyandcurly@gmail.com

Stay tuned to Lizzy Armentrout on Facebook and Instagram to be updated about the next adventure in the Shelly Gale series!

Blessings,

Lizzy

Psalm 28:7

The Lord is my strength and my shield;
my heart trusts in him, and he helps me.
My heart leaps for joy,
and with my song I praise him.

Author

LIZZY ARMENTROUT

Author Lizzy Armentrout, formerly of King, North Carolina, is currently living her best life in Fort Myers, Florida. She graduated with a Bachelor of Science degree in Elementary Education from Piedmont Bible College and was a teacher for twenty-eight years. Now retired and disabled, she spends her time reading, writing, and participating in her local church.

She would love to connect with you:
Facebook: @ShellyGaleMysteries
Instagram: @lizzyarmentrout
Email: shellyandcurly@gmail.com